1934

CHANGES FOR KIT

A Winter Story

BY VALERIE TRIPP

ILLUSTRATIONS WALTER RANE

VIGNETTES SUSAN MCALILEY

American Girl®

Published by Pleasant Company Publications
Copyright © 2001 by Pleasant Company

Printed in the United States of America.
01 02 03 04 05 06 07 08 QWT 12 11 10 9 8 7 6 5 4 3 2 1

The American Girls Collection®, Kit®, Kit Kittredge®, and American Girl®
are registered trademarks of Pleasant Company.

PICTURE CREDITS

The following individuals and organizations have generously given
permission to reprint images contained in "Looking Back":
pp. 60–61—Photograph Copyright © 2001: Whitney Museum of American Art
(*Employment Agency*, by Isaac Soyer); Library of Congress, LC-USF33-012949-M1 (sweeping girls);
© Underwood & Underwood/CORBIS (bank line); Franklin D. Roosevelt Library (FDR);
pp. 62–63—© Bettmann/CORBIS (suntanned starlets, NRA poster, WPA mural painter);
© CORBIS (women painters poster); National Archives Photo No. 69-N-2284 (puppet maker);
Library of Congress (cartoon); pp. 64–65—© Bettmann/CORBIS (Eleanor Roosevelt in coal mine);
© CORBIS (three children and coats); Franklin D. Roosevelt Library (dust storm);
Library of Congress LC-USF34-016459-E (migrant girl with baby);
pp. 66–67—Hugo Jaeger/TimePix (Hitler); © Hulton-Deutsch Collection/CORBIS
(munitions workers); © Bettmann/CORBIS (Pearl Harbor attack, war correspondent);
© Bettmann/CORBIS (*New York Journal*); © Francis G. Mayer/CORBIS (*New York Times*);
printed by permission of the Norman Rockwell Family Trust, © 1943 Norman Rockwell
Family Trust/CORBIS (*Freedom from Want*, by Norman Rockwell).

Cover Background Illustration by Paul Bachem

Library of Congress Cataloging-in-Publication Data

Tripp, Valerie, 1951–
Changes for Kit : a winter story / by Valerie Tripp ;
illustrations, Walter Rane ; vignettes, Susan McAliley.

p. cm. — (The American girls collection)

Summary: In 1934, during the Depression, Kit's cantankerous uncle comes
to live in the Cincinnati boardinghouse run by her parents, enlisting her aid
in transcribing his complaining letters to the editor of the local newspaper,
and inspiring her to write a different kind of letter of her own.

ISBN 1-58485-027-2 (hc.). — ISBN 1-58485-026-4 (pbk.)
1. Depressions—1929—Juvenile fiction.
[1. Depressions—1929—Fiction. 2. Authorship—Fiction. 3. Boardinghouses—Fiction.
4. Uncles—Fiction. 5. Conduct of life—Fiction. 6. Cincinnati (Ohio)—Fiction.]
I. Rane, Walter, ill. II. McAliley, Susan, ill. III. Title. IV. Series.
PZ7.T7363 Cgh 2001 [Fic]—dc21 2001021312

FOR MY MOTHER, KATHLEEN MARTIN TRIPP,
WHO INSPIRED BOTH KIT AND ME, WITH
LOVE AND THANKS

TABLE OF CONTENTS

KIT'S FAMILY
AND FRIENDS

DAD
*Kit's father, a
businessman facing
the problems of the
Great Depression.*

MOTHER
*Kit's mother, who takes
care of her family and
their home with strength
and determination.*

KIT
*A clever, resourceful
girl who helps her family
cope with the dark days
of the Depression.*

CHARLIE
*Kit's affectionate
and supportive
older brother.*

**UNCLE
HENDRICK**
*Mother's wealthy and
disapproving uncle.*

MRS. HOWARD
*Mother's garden club
friend, who is a guest in
the Kittredge home.*

**STIRLING
HOWARD**
*Mrs. Howard's son,
whose delicate health
hides surprising
strengths.*

**RUTHIE
SMITHENS**
*Kit's best friend, who
is loyal, understanding,
and generous.*

SOMETHING WONDERFUL

 Something wonderful was going to
happen. Kit Kittredge knew it the
minute she and her friends Ruthie and
Stirling walked in the door after school.

Mother was waiting for them in the front hall.
"Here you are at last," she said, sounding cheerfully
impatient. "Hang up your coats. Then come join me
in the living room."

Mother left, and Kit turned to Ruthie and
Stirling. "I wonder what's up," she whispered.

Ruthie shrugged and Stirling said, "Who
knows?" But Kit saw them slip sly smiles to each
other, so she knew they were in cahoots with
Mother.

The children hurriedly hung up their coats, took off their boots, and rushed into the living room. Stirling's mother, Mrs. Howard, was there looking happy and fluttery. Kit's older brother, Charlie, had a smile a mile wide. Miss Hart and Miss Finney, two nurses who were boarders in the Kittredges' house, simply beamed. Even Grace, Kit's dog, wore a goofy, drooly, doggy grin. But no one looked happier than Mother as she came toward Kit.

"This is for you, dear," Mother said. She was holding a winter coat. It was made of dark gray wool tweed flecked with blue. It had deep pockets and cuffs, four big buttons, and a belt.

"Wow," breathed Kit.

"Try it on!" said Ruthie. "See how it fits."

"Yes," insisted everyone. "Go ahead."

Kit hesitated. "It's a beautiful coat," she said. "I really like it. But . . ."

Kit knew her family didn't have a penny to spare. Her father had lost his business almost two years ago because of the Depression. Ever since then, they'd had to struggle to pay the mortgage on their house every month. Kit asked, "Isn't a new coat like this awfully expensive?"

Much to Kit's surprise, everyone laughed.

"This coat isn't new," said Mother. "It belonged to Dad."

Mrs. Howard piped up. "Your mother and I took his old coat apart, washed the material, cut it to size, and made a new coat for you using the material inside out," she said proudly. "Wasn't that clever of us?"

"It sure was," agreed Kit, who believed that her mother was the cleverest mother in the world. It had been Mother's idea to turn their home into a boarding house. She had made a go of it in spite of hard times and the disapproval of her rich, grumpy old Uncle Hendrick, who was sure it would be a disaster. There were five boarders now: Miss Hart and Miss Finney, a musician named Mr. Peck, and Stirling and his mother. Aunt Millie and the Bells had left. The rent the boarders paid helped the Kittredges make ends meet, though they still had to be very thrifty. Kit grinned. "I like the coat even more knowing that it's not exactly new," she said.

"Good," said Miss Hart. "Then you'll like our surprise, too." She winked at Miss Finney and Ruthie.

"Ta da!" sang Miss Finney. She and Ruthie presented Kit with a knitted red hat and blue-and-red mittens.

"These aren't exactly new, either," Ruthie said. "The red yarn came from an old sweater of Stirling's that we unraveled, and the blue yarn came from a cap of Charlie's that Grace chewed."

"Unfortunately, Grace and I have the same taste in caps," said Charlie. He crossed his arms over his chest and pretended to frown down at Grace. But Grace, far from looking ashamed, seemed pleased with herself for her part in the creation of the mittens. She thumped her tail importantly.

"Go on, Kit," said Ruthie. "We're dying to see how everything looks."

Mother held the coat as Kit slipped her arms into the sleeves. Then Kit buttoned the buttons, buckled the belt, and pulled on the mittens and the hat.

"The hat goes like this," said Mother, tilting Kit's hat *just so*. "There," she said. "Perfect. Now turn around so we can see the whole effect."

Kit spun around. Charlie whistled, Stirling clapped, and all the ladies *oohed* and *aahed*. Kit blushed. She felt a little bashful about being the center of attention. But she knew that everyone was glad to have an excuse to make a happy fuss. Back before the Depression began, when her family had plenty of money, no one would have carried on much about a new coat. Now it was something to celebrate.

"Oh, look!" said Mrs. Howard. "Everything fits like a dream."

"And it's so stylish!" added Miss Finney.

"The coat makes you look really tall, Kit," said Ruthie with an approving air. "The whole outfit is very grown-up."

"I love it," Kit said. "Thank you, every one of you. It's wonderful. All of it." Kit held the collar to her nose and took a deep, delicious breath of the clean-smelling, woolly material. She felt warm and cozy, all the more so because the coat and hat and mittens had been made for her by her friends and family out of things that had belonged to them. It was as if affection had been sewn into the seams of the stout wool coat and knitted into the hat and mittens to cover Kit with warmth from head to toe. She sighed a sigh of pure pleasure. "It was very nice of all of you to make these things for me," she said.

"Well, you desperately needed a new coat," said Mother. "Your old coat has been too small for two years now."

Kit had a sudden thought. "Mother," she asked, "do we need my old coat? Are you planning to take it apart and make something out of *it*, too?"

"Why, no," answered Mother. "I don't think so."

"Then may I give it away?" asked Kit. She explained, "I keep thinking about the children Stirling and I saw in the hobo jungle last summer. This cold weather must be terrible for them." The summer before, Kit and Stirling had gone to the hobo jungle, which was the place by the railroad tracks where hoboes camped. Kit had been surprised and saddened to see a whole family there, with little children. Many times since then she'd wished she could do something for those hobo children. Their shoes were so worn out and their clothes were so thin and ragged! Now she asked Mother, "Would it be all right if Stirling and Ruthie and I went to the jungle this afternoon? Maybe there's a girl there who could use my old coat."

"I think that's a very good idea," said Mother.

She turned to Mrs. Howard and asked, "Is it all right with you if Stirling goes, too?"

Mrs. Howard nodded. "As long as they stay away from the trains," she said, "and come home before dark."

"We'll be back in time to do our chores before dinner," Kit promised.

"Hurry along, then," said Mother. "And Ruthie, be sure to stop by your house and ask your mother for permission to go."

"I will!" said Ruthie.

Kit folded her old coat over her arm as Ruthie and Stirling put their coats and boots back on. Then the children went outside, bundled up against the February afternoon. Kit smiled. She hardly felt the cold, snug as she was in her not-exactly-new, wonderful winter coat, hat, and mittens!

Ruthie's mother gave Ruthie permission to go. She also gave the children a sack of potatoes for the hoboes. The children took turns carrying the sack as they walked through town and past the front of Union Station. Kit was sure of the way. But when they came to the spot next to the river where the hobo jungle had been during the summer, it was deserted.

"Where'd the jungle go?" asked Stirling.

"Are you sure we're in the right place?" asked Ruthie.

Kit looked around. Not one tired hobo was lying asleep on the ground with his hat over his face, or resting his weary feet, or repairing his travel-worn shoes. There were no tents or rickety lean-tos propped against the trees, no hungry children eating stew, no clothes spread on the bushes to dry as there'd been in the summer. There was no fire inside the circle of stones on the windswept, bare ground, no scent of coffee, no music. All was oddly quiet.

"Hey," said Stirling. "Look."

He pointed, and Kit and Ruthie saw smoke rising up, dark gray like a pencil squiggle against the pale winter sky. The smoke was coming straight out of the ground! Kit looked more closely and saw that someone had dug a cavelike shelter into the embankment under the bridge. There was even a door built into the hillside.

"Come on," Kit said. She knocked on the door.

A man with a weather-beaten face opened it. "Yes?" he asked. His gruff voice reminded Kit of stern Uncle Hendrick.

"Excuse me, sir," Kit said politely. "But where are all the hoboes?"

"Someplace south, if they're smart," said the man. "There are five of us living in this cave and we don't have room for any more."

"But what about the ones who are riding the rails?" asked Kit. "Lots of people camped here last summer when they were passing through town."

"Humph!" harrumphed the man. "Don't you know that this is Cincinnati's coldest winter in twenty-nine years? Folks'd freeze to death camping out. Most hoboes who are passing through go to soup kitchens or missions. Sometimes they can stay for a night or two if they do chores. Then they have to move on."

"Oh, I see," said Kit. She thanked the man, and Ruthie gave him the sack of potatoes. Then Kit, Stirling, and Ruthie walked to the soup kitchen on River Street. They'd once delivered a Thanksgiving basket of food there, so they knew to go to the back door to make their delivery. They went inside and carefully made their way past the stoves steaming with pots of soup, around the busy people making sandwiches and coffee, and through the swinging door to the front part of the soup kitchen where the food was served.

The three children stopped still and stared at the crowded room. An endless line of men, women, and children shuffled in the front door and past the tables where soup, bread, and coffee were served. Every seat at every table was taken, so many people had to eat standing up. Groups of people, grim and gray, were gathered in the corners. Families huddled together wherever they could and spoke in low murmurs. Somewhere a baby was crying. *So many people,* thought Kit sadly, *young and old, and all so hungry and poor.*

Kit knew that only luck and chance separated her family from those she saw around her. Almost two years ago her own father had come to this very soup kitchen to get food for her family because he had run out of money. That year they fell so far behind in paying the mortgage that they would have been evicted—thrown out of their house—if Dad's

So many people, thought Kit sadly, young and old,
and all so hungry and poor.

Aunt Millie had not rescued them with her life savings. Things were better for Kit's family now. But the Depression had taught Kit that nothing was certain. Everything could change suddenly, and she could find herself standing in line for soup, just like these children.

It made Kit's heart hurt to see them. One child was wearing a filthy, worn-out, threadbare coat that was much too small. Another wore a ragged overcoat that dragged on the ground. One even wore a blanket tied around his waist with rope. Their shoes were even worse. Some of the children had nothing but rags wrapped around their feet. Others wore broken-down boots with no laces, rubber galoshes they'd lined with old newspapers, or too-small shoes with the front part cut so that their toes poked out.

Ruthie tugged on Kit's sleeve. She nodded her head toward an area where people were sitting on the floor, leaning against the wall. "There's someone who needs your coat," she said.

At first, all Kit could see was what looked like a pile of dirty rags. But then she saw a little girl's thin, pinched face above the rags, and she realized that the rags were the little girl's skimpy coat—or what was left of it. It was badly stained and torn. The pockets had been ripped off and used to patch the elbows, and all the buttons but one were gone. The little girl was cuddled up to her mother. Her hair was tangled, her eyes were dull, and she seemed as lifeless and colorless as a shadow.

Kit, Ruthie, and Stirling went over and quietly stood in front of the girl and her mother. Kit held out her old coat. "Ma'am," she said to the mother, "may I give this coat to your little girl?"

The woman didn't answer. She looked at Kit as if she didn't quite believe what she had heard. But the little girl stood up. Shyly, eagerly, she took the coat from Kit and put it on over her ragged one. She smoothed the front of the coat with both hands, and then she raised her face to Kit. In that moment, something wonderful happened. The little girl was transformed from a ghost to a real girl. She hugged herself, and her pale cheeks glowed. "Thank you," she said to Kit, smiling a smile that lit her whole face.

Kit smiled back. "You're very welcome," she said. She could tell that the little girl felt the same way *she* had felt about *her* new coat. It warmed her both inside and out.

Bright, brilliant streaks of pink and purple were splashed across the late-afternoon sky as Kit, Ruthie, and Stirling walked home from the soup kitchen.

"Kit, you were like the fairy godmother who turned Cinderella's rags into a ball gown," said Ruthie, who liked fairy tales. "You gave that girl your old coat and *whoosh*." She waved an imaginary wand. "You changed her."

"Maybe," said Kit. "But that was just one coat and just one kid. Every kid there needed a coat— and shoes."

"Those poor kids," said Ruthie, "having to sleep on the floor! It's terrible that there's no better place for them to stay. Isn't there *anywhere* their parents could look for help?"

"I think," said Stirling, "they *are* looking for help. That's why they're on the road. Maybe they heard about jobs in New York or California. Or maybe they ran out of money and lost their homes, so they're traveling to friends or family, hoping to be taken in. They don't have any money for train fare, so they have to ride the rails. They can't pay for a hotel, so they eat and sleep at soup kitchens for a day or two. Then they're on their way again."

"In the freezing cold," added Kit. "In their ragged coats and worn-out shoes." She sighed. If only she had a hundred coats to give away, and a hundred pairs of shoes. *That* would be wonderful.

Kit and Stirling said good-bye to Ruthie at the end of her driveway and arrived home just as dusk fell. Kit went straight to work doing her evening chores. As she fed the dog and the chickens, scrubbed potatoes, and set the table for dinner, she remembered the hobo in his cheerless cave and the people in the crowded soup kitchen. *How lucky I am,* she thought. Her house might not be fancy. In fact, it was getting rather shabby. But it was warm and filled with good-hearted people who cared for one another.

Dinner was jolly that night. Afterward, Mr. Peck played his bass fiddle and Charlie played the piano. They made "Music to Do the Dishes By," and every-one sang along. Mother never used to allow the boarders to help clean up, but she had relaxed a bit

and treated them more like family now. Stirling
and Mrs. Howard sang as they cleared the table.
Miss Hart and Miss Finney chimed in as they helped
Mother wash the dishes. And Dad and Kit sang in
harmony as they dried. Grace, who never liked to be
left out, howled.

They were making so much noise that they
didn't hear Mr. Smithens, Ruthie's father, knocking
on the front door. They were surprised when he
stepped into the kitchen.

"Excuse me, folks," Mr. Smithens said. "I'm
sorry to barge in. But we had a call for you on our

telephone." The Kittredges could not afford a
telephone, so the Smithenses kindly took calls for
them. "It was Cincinnati Hospital," Mr. Smithens
said to Mother and Dad. "It seems that your
Uncle Hendrick had a fall and broke his ankle and
his wrist. They've patched him up, and he's fine.
But the nurse said he's making quite a ruckus. He
wants you to come immediately and pick him up
and bring him back here so that you can care for
him until he's back on his feet. I'll drive you to the
hospital as soon as you're ready to go."

"Thank you, Stan," said Dad. "We'll be right
with you."

Mother had already taken off her apron and put
on her hat and coat. In a minute, she and Dad were
gone. The door closed behind them, and Kit stood
in the sudden silence in the chilly front hall. *Oh no,*
she thought, her heart sinking lower and lower as
the news sank in. *Cranky, crabby, cantankerous Uncle
Hendrick is coming to stay in our house. It'll be terrible.*

CHAPTER
TWO
—
TO DO

"We've got to think of *something* to write," said Kit.

It was Saturday morning, and Kit, Ruthie, and Stirling were up in Kit's attic room, sitting around her typewriter. They were working on a newspaper. Before the Depression, Kit used to make newspapers for her father to tell him what had happened at home while he was away at work all day. Now that her family took in boarders, Kit made newspapers so that everyone in the household knew what was going on. When new boarders arrived, Kit always made a special newspaper to welcome them and to introduce them to the other boarders.

Usually, Kit's head was so full of things to write that her fingers couldn't move fast enough on the typewriter keys to keep up. In this case, however, the new boarders were Uncle Hendrick and his stinky dog, Inky. They'd been living with the Kittredges for more than a week, and so far, they had not endeared themselves to anyone. Even Grace, who liked *everybody* and lavished slobbery affection on complete strangers, kept her distance from Inky and showed a cool indifference to Uncle Hendrick. Kit couldn't think of anything to write about them that was both enthusiastic and honest.

"You could take a photograph of Uncle Hendrick," suggested Stirling. Kit had an old camera that her brother, Charlie, had fixed for her, and she was eager to use it. "A picture tells more about a person than words ever could."

"Maybe, but it costs money to get the film developed," said Kit, "so I was kind of hoping to take pictures of things I really liked."

"How about a drawing?" said Ruthie. "You're a good artist, Stirling. You could draw a picture of Uncle Hendrick."

19

"And Inky, too," added Kit.

"All right," said Stirling, opening up his sketch-pad. "Under my drawing I'll write, 'His bark is worse than his bite.'"

"Whose?" asked Ruthie, looking impish. "Inky's or Uncle Hendrick's?"

Kit smiled weakly at Ruthie's joke. Personally, she thought Uncle Hendrick's biting remarks were just as bad as the orders he barked at her.

Caring for Uncle Hendrick had turned out to be Kit's job. Mother was much too busy, and Dad had a part-time job at the airport. Charlie helped out while Kit was at school. But when she was home, Uncle Hendrick and Inky were her responsibility, and they were a big one.

Uncle Hendrick said he couldn't go up and down the stairs because of his ankle. Before school, Kit had to bring him his morning newspaper and his breakfast tray. She also had to walk Inky. Uncle Hendrick dozed all day, so when Kit came home from school, he was fully awake, full of pepper and vinegar, and full of demands and commands. He always made a big To Do list for Kit. Then he made

a big speech about how to do everything on the
To Do list. Then he made a big to-do about how
she had done everything wrong on yesterday's
To Do list.

And tasks and errands were not all. Uncle
Hendrick grew bored sitting in his room with
no one but Inky for company. He expected Kit
to entertain him. During the first few days,
Charlie had helped by playing checkers
with Uncle Hendrick. But Charlie had
won too often, and now Uncle Hendrick
didn't want to play checkers with him anymore. He preferred badgering Kit. His idea of a
conversation was to snap at her, "What's the capital
of Maine?" or, "How much is seven percent of three
hundred ninety-two?" Having Uncle Hendrick in
the house was every bit as terrible as Kit had
thought it would be.

"Let's just write in our newspaper that we're
sorry Uncle Hendrick hurt his ankle and his wrist,
and we hope he is better soon," said Stirling.

"That's good," said Kit. She swiveled her chair
around to face the desk and began *clickety-clacking*
away on her old black typewriter. "And it's true,

because the sooner he's better, the sooner he and Inky can go home!"

"The headline could be, 'The Sooner, The Better!'" joked Ruthie.

Suddenly, *bang, bang, bang!* A thunderous thumping shook the floor under the children's feet. It was accompanied by ferocious barking.

"Yikes!" said Ruthie, covering her ears. "What's *that?*"

"That's Uncle Hendrick calling me," said Kit. "He whacks his ceiling with his cane and then Inky barks. I'd better go see what they want."

"Go!" said Ruthie. "Stirling and I will finish up the newspaper."

"Thanks," said Kit. She gave up her chair to Ruthie, then pelted down the stairs and poked her head into Uncle Hendrick's room. "Do you need me, Uncle Hendrick?" she asked, shouting to be heard.

Uncle Hendrick stopped walloping the ceiling. Inky stopped barking, but threw in a few extra yips and growls for good measure. "What on earth was that infernal racket coming from upstairs?" asked Uncle Hendrick crossly.

"The headline could be, 'The Sooner, The Better!'" joked Ruthie.

Privately, Kit thought that Uncle Hendrick and Inky were the ones who'd made the racket. But she answered politely, "I was typing. Ruthie and Stirling and I are making a newspaper."

"What a waste of time," Uncle Hendrick snorted. "Making a pretend newspaper. Writing nonsense! Haven't you outgrown such silly childishness?"

Kit lifted her chin. She was rather proud of her newspapers. She never wrote nonsense. She loved writing, respected words, and tried hard to find the perfect ones to use, which was not the least bit childish to do. Now, for example, the perfect word to describe how she felt would be *annoyed*.

But Uncle Hendrick didn't notice her annoyance. As usual, he was concerned only about what he wanted. "Sit down!" he ordered. "I'll give you something worthwhile to write. Take a letter!"

Uncle Hendrick had broken the wrist on his right hand—his writing hand—so when he wanted to send a letter, he had to dictate it to Kit. Sometimes Kit thought that Uncle Hendrick had named his dog "Inky" because ink was something he liked to use so much. Almost every day, Uncle Hendrick dictated a letter. Usually it was a letter to the editor of the newspaper. And usually it was about "that man in the White House," which was what Uncle Hendrick called President Franklin Delano Roosevelt. Uncle Hendrick did not approve of FDR, which was what most people called the president. He did not like FDR's wife, Eleanor, either. As far as he was concerned, everything that was wrong with the country was their fault. Today Uncle Hendrick's angry letter was in response to a newspaper article he'd read about the programs FDR had started as part of the National Recovery Administration to fight the Depression.

President and Mrs. Roosevelt

"To the Editor," Uncle Hendrick began as soon as Kit was seated with pen and paper. "The NRA is a waste of taxpayers' money. It creates useless, make-work jobs so the government can hand out money to lazy idlers. FDR is drowning the USA in his alphabet soup of NRA programs, such as the CCC and the CWA."

Kit shifted in her chair. Uncle Hendrick knew perfectly well that last year Charlie had worked for the CCC, or Civilian Conservation Corps, in Montana for six months. Every month, Charlie had sent home twenty-five of the thirty dollars he earned. Her family had depended on it. Charlie liked his experience in the CCC so much that he hoped to sign up again. Uncle Hendrick also knew that the Civil Works Administration, or CWA, had given Dad the first job he'd had in almost two years. It was just a short-term, part-time, low-paying job clearing land and building stone walls out at the airport. But Dad was glad to be working again. Kit loved seeing him go off to work, whistling and cheerful. He was proud of his work, and he thought it might lead to a better job that would use his skills as a mechanic. The other day at the hangar he'd met an old friend named Mr. Hesse who'd said that soon there might be work repairing airplane engines.

Kit pressed her lips together as Uncle Hendrick went on saying critical things about the very programs that were helping her family. "In short," Uncle Hendrick wound up, "when I say 'that man in the White House' is going to be the ruination of our fine country, all must agree."

I don't, thought Kit. But she kept her opinion to

herself. She had learned that it was useless to argue with Uncle Hendrick. It was best to concentrate on keeping up with him and writing exactly what he said without misspelling any words. If the letter was not perfect, Uncle Hendrick pounced on the mistakes and ordered Kit to copy the whole thing over again. He was a stickler.

Kit handed him the letter. He read it, gave a curt nod of approval, then took the pen and signed it as well as he could with his hand in a cast. "They don't print unsigned letters," he said. "Now, deliver this to Mr. Gibson at the newspaper offices immediately. No lollygagging!"

"Yes, sir," said Kit. Uncle Hendrick always acted as if the newspaper editor was waiting breathlessly for his letter and couldn't send the newspaper to press without it. He was absolutely confident that his letter would be printed. And rightly so, it seemed, because many of his letters did appear in the newspaper. Kit thought it was because he was rich and important. But she had to admit that though she disagreed with what he said, she admired how he said it. Uncle Hendrick expressed his opinions forcefully. He never wasted a word. He said precisely what he meant, with lots of vim and vigor.

Ruthie had left, and Stirling was busy drawing a picture of Kit in her new coat for their newspaper. So Kit went off on her errand alone. She knew the way well: down the hill, past the beautiful fountain in the center of the city, over two blocks and up one. The newspaper offices were not far from the soup kitchen. Kit saw lots of children in ragged coats and pitiful shoes, but not the little girl to whom she had given her coat. She hoped the girl and her mother were home, or at least someplace safe and warm and comfortable.

Kit smiled as she went inside the big brick building that housed the newspaper offices. She climbed the stairs briskly, her footsteps *tsk-tsking* as she did. She could just imagine how Uncle Hendrick would  *tsk-tsk* and sniff disdainfully if he knew how she loved to pretend that she was a reporter who worked in this building. She pushed open the door to the newsroom and was greeted with the clamor of telephones ringing, typewriters clacking, and people chatting. The noisy newsroom seemed like heaven to

Kit. *This is where the newspaper is created,* she thought. *Stories that thousands of people will read are being written right here, right now.*

As she walked through the room to Mr. Gibson's desk, several people nodded to her. She'd delivered letters to the newspaper offices so many times that her face was familiar. Some of the friendlier reporters even knew her name. "Hi, Kit," one said as she passed by. "Got another letter for Gibb?"

"Yes, I do," Kit said. She knew they all called Mr. Gibson, the editor, "Gibb."

Gibb was not very friendly. He sat frowning

behind his messy, cluttered desk. When Kit came near, he said without enthusiasm, "Put it in the box." He never even looked up.

"Yes, sir," said Kit. She put Uncle Hendrick's letter in Gibb's in-box on top of lots of other letters and a few rolls of film. Then she turned to go.

Kit wished she could linger in the newsroom. How she'd love to talk to the reporters! But she knew she had better hurry home to her chores. Saturday was the day she always washed all the sheets and put fresh ones on the boarders' beds. It also was the day she and Stirling went around the neighborhood selling eggs. After that, it would be time to help Mother with dinner. Kit was proud of the way she did her chores these days with great efficiency. *I bet I can find time to put the finishing touches on our newspaper,* she thought, *unless Uncle Hendrick has thought up something else for me to do.*

CHAPTER
THREE
—

LETTERS WITH
AN 'S'

On the last Sunday in February, Kit
was trotting past the door to Uncle
Hendrick's room with a laundry basket
full of her clean clothes propped on her hip when
she heard Uncle Hendrick call her.

"Kit, come here!" he barked. Inky barked, too,
then followed up with a wheezy whine.

Kit stuck her head in the door. "Yes, sir?" she
asked.

"Take a letter!" said Uncle Hendrick.

Not now! Kit thought. She'd been rushing to
finish her chores ever since going out in the eerie
early-morning light to get Uncle Hendrick's newspaper. Today was a special day. After lunch, Dad's

friend Mr. Hesse was going to drive Dad and Kit
and Charlie to the airport. Kit had already carefully
put her camera in her coat pocket because she
wanted to photograph Dad standing next to some
of the stone walls he'd built. She also hoped Charlie
would take *her* picture posed next to an airplane,
just like her heroine, the pilot Amelia Earhart.
Mother had said that Kit could use some of the egg
money to have the film developed.

Reluctantly, Kit lowered the laundry basket,
entered Uncle Hendrick's room, and picked up the
pen and paper. She hoped the letter would be short.

"Start by writing, 'To the Editor,'" Uncle
Hendrick instructed Kit, precisely as he had done
many times before. Then he cleared his throat and
dictated, "This morning I read on page twenty-five
of your newspaper that an empty
hospital in Covington, across the river
from Cincinnati, may be used as a
home for transients and unemployed persons."

Kit looked up. "Really?" she asked. "What a
great idea!"

"Quiet!" growled Uncle Hendrick, echoed by
Inky. Uncle Hendrick went on dictating, "This is an

outrage! Such a home will attract tramps and drifters from all over the country. They'll flock here to be housed, fed, and clothed at our expense. We'll be pampering worthless riffraff. All of these hoboes are men who have chosen to wander rather than work."

"Excuse me, Uncle Hendrick," Kit interrupted. She usually didn't say anything. But this time she had to speak up. "That's not true."

"I beg your pardon?" asked Uncle Hendrick icily.

"It's not true that all of the hoboes are men who have chosen to wander instead of working," Kit said. "Lots of them are on the road because they lost their jobs and their homes and they're trying to find work. And not all of the hoboes are men, either. Some are teenagers out on their own, some are women, and there are even whole families with little children."

Uncle Hendrick frowned at Kit. "Not another word out of you, Miss Impertinence," he said. "Write what I say. Keep your comments to yourself."

"Yes, sir," said Kit. She kept silent while Uncle Hendrick dictated the rest of his letter. But inside, she disagreed with every word.

"There!" said Uncle Hendrick, signing the letter. "Deliver this today."

Kit's heart sank as she took the letter. "But Uncle Hendrick," she protested. "I'm going to the airport with Dad and Charlie to take photos."

"No, you're not," said Uncle Hendrick, not the least bit sorry to be the bearer of bad news. "Mrs. Smithens came over earlier to tell your father that Mr. Hesse called. He doesn't want to drive anywhere because of the snow."

Kit looked out at the murky mid-morning sky. Snow was falling in a determined manner, as if it meant business. She sighed.

"Do as I say and deliver that letter," said Uncle Hendrick. "And do as I say and forget that nonsense you were blathering about earlier, too."

"It isn't nonsense," Kit insisted hotly, standing up to her uncle for once. "It's true. Hoboes are just poor people who are down on their luck."

"That," said Uncle Hendrick in a superior tone, "is just the kind of poppycock I'd expect your soft-headed parents to tell you."

It made Kit furious when Uncle Hendrick

criticized her parents. "No one told me that," she said. "I learned it myself. I've been to the hobo jungle and to a soup kitchen, too."

"Whatever for?" asked Uncle Hendrick. He looked at Kit with unconcealed horror. "Hoboes are thieves and beggars. Why go near them?"

"I want to help," Kit said simply. "Especially the children."

"Ha!" scoffed Uncle Hendrick so loudly that Kit jumped and Inky yipped. "You're nothing but a child yourself, still caught up in babyish play, like making newspapers! What help could *you* be?" He raised his eyebrows. "I suppose you're planning to end the Depression single-handedly, is that it?"

"No, of course not," Kit said, hating how Uncle Hendrick made her feel so foolish, flushed, and flustered. "I don't mean that. I know I can't change much by myself. Not me alone." She tried to settle her rattled thoughts and speak sensibly. "I just think that if people knew about the hobo children, if they saw how terrible the children's coats and shoes are, I'm sure they'd help," she said. "And then the children would know that people cared about them, and that would give them hope, and—"

"I suppose you're planning to end the Depression single-handedly, is that it?"

"Hope!" Uncle Hendrick cut in sharply. "An empty word. Comfort for fools. Hope never put a nickel in anybody's pocket, my girl, and hope is not going to end the Depression. Neither is pouring money into useless programs, or handing out coats or shoes to hobo children!" He dismissed Kit with a backward flutter of his hand, as if brushing away a tiresome fly. "Off with you," he said. "I, just like everyone else in the world, have better things to do than to listen to the jibber-jabber of a silly child like *you*. Go."

Kit left. She put Uncle Hendrick's letter in the laundry basket, wearily hoisted the basket onto her hip, then slowly trudged upstairs to her attic. Once there, she did not even have the energy to put her clothes away. Instead, she plunked down at her desk. Never had she felt so discouraged. Never had she felt such despair.

For almost two years, ever since Dad lost his job, she and her family had struggled through ups and downs, believing that if they worked hard enough, things would change for the better—not just for their family but for everyone hit hard by the Depression.

It was that hope that kept them going. If Uncle Hendrick was right, if hope was for fools, what did they have left? The Depression had won, and there was nothing anyone could do. There was certainly nothing *she* could do to change anything. Uncle Hendrick had made that clear to her.

Tears welled in Kit's eyes. She put one elbow on either side of her typewriter and held her head in her hands. She sniffed hard, trying not to cry. Then she took a deep, shaky breath. Somehow, the dark, inky smell of the typewriter ribbon just under her nose comforted her, and so did the solid, clunky black bulk of the typewriter itself. Next to the typewriter, Kit saw the drawing Stirling had made for their newspaper. He'd drawn her striding along, her camera slung around her neck, wearing her new coat. *Chipper*, she said to herself. *That is the perfect word to describe how I look in Stirling's drawing. And what would be the perfect word to describe how I feel now? Crushed? Flattened? No. Squashed.* Idly, Kit touched the **s** key. She remembered how Dad had fixed it when the typewriter was broken. He had repaired the typewriter for her because he knew how much writing meant to her. Kit pushed down hard on the **s** and the key struck the paper with a satisfying *whack*, a sound that Kit loved.

Kit sat bolt upright. Suddenly, she knew what she must do: write!

If Uncle Hendrick could write letters to the newspaper, she could, too. She might not be rich or important, but she knew how to write a letter that said what she wanted it to say. She'd deliver her letter right along with Uncle Hendrick's. It might not appear in the newspaper, it might not change anything or anyone else, but writing it would change the way she felt.

Quickly, Kit rolled the paper with the **s** on it out of the typewriter so she could write her rough draft on the back of it. She picked up her pencil. *Now,* she thought, *how should I begin?* Then Kit grinned. "To the Editor," she wrote. Wasn't that what Uncle Hendrick had taught her? Hadn't he, in fact, taught her exactly how to write a letter to the newspaper? How many times had he said that a letter must have one point to make and must make it in simple, direct language, using not more than two hundred and fifty words? Hadn't he told her over and over again that letters must be signed or they wouldn't be printed?

Without intending to, Uncle Hendrick had been a very helpful teacher because of all his hectoring and fusspot bossiness.

And Uncle Hendrick was not the only one helping Kit. As she wrote, she thought of Dad's dignity, Mother's industriousness, and the cheerful good nature of the boarders. She thought of Charlie, who'd come back from Montana with his "muscles grown hard, back grown strong, and heart grown stout," just as it said in the CCC booklet. She thought of steadfast Stirling, funny Ruthie, and how kind and neighborly Ruthie's family had been to hers. She thought about thrifty, ingenious Aunt Millie, who saved their house with her generosity; Will, the young hobo who had taught her about courage; and the little girl at the soup kitchen who'd brightened with hope when Kit gave her the old coat. Thinking about the way each one battled the Depression, its losses and fears, gave strength to what Kit wrote.

Kit worked on her letter for a long time. She chose her words carefully. She formed sentences in her head, then wrote and rewrote them till they sounded right. Then she read her rough draft aloud to herself:

To the Editor:

I think it is a good idea to use the hospital in Covington as a home to house, feed, and clothe hoboes. I have met some hoboes, and they are not all the same. Every hobo has his or her own story. Some hoboes chose a wandering life. Some people are hoboes because they lost their jobs and their homes and have nowhere to go. Some hoboes are grownups, some are young people, and there are even hobo families with little children. Though they all have different reasons for being on the road, I think all hoboes hope the road they're on will lead them to better times. But it is a long, hard trip, and they have nowhere to stay on the way. I think they deserve our help, sympathy, and compassion.

Hobo life is especially hard on children. They are often hungry and cold. Their coats and shoes are worn-out and outgrown. It would be a big help if people donated coats and shoes for children to soup kitchens and missions. It would show the children that we care about them, and that would give them hope. It would give all of us hope, too, because it would be a change for the better. Sometimes hope is all any of us, hoboes or not, have to go on.

Margaret Mildred Kittredge
Cincinnati, Ohio

Kit was pretty sure she had spelled *compassion* right. But something looked fishy about *sympathy*, and she didn't know whether *outgrown* was one word or two. Uncle Hendrick always said that there was no excuse for lazy spellers, and that a misspelled word made your reader lose confidence in you. So Kit looked up both *sympathy* and *outgrown* in the dictionary. When she was positive her spelling and punctuation were correct, she typed her letter very carefully. She struck every key hard, and with conviction. This time, Kit didn't care if the type-writer was noisy. Uncle Hendrick could hit the ceiling and Inky could howl and yowl. They were not going to stop her.

But there was no bluster or banging from below, and Kit was able to finish her letter in peace. She was folding it to put it into an envelope when Ruthie and Stirling came up the attic stairs.

"Hey, Kit," said Ruthie. "Want to come with Stirling and me? I've got some shoes and coats that're too small for me, and we're bringing them to the soup kitchen."

42

"Sure," said Kit. "Then after, I have some letters to deliver to the newspaper office."

"Letters with an 's'?" asked Stirling. "You mean Uncle Hendrick dictated two today?"

Kit smiled. "No," she said. "One is mine."

CHAPTER
FOUR
—

THE PERFECT
WORD

As they walked to the soup kitchen, Kit told Ruthie and Stirling about her argument with Uncle Hendrick and her decision to write a letter of her own. "I had to," she said. "Not just because I think he's wrong about the hoboes, but also because I felt so terrible when he said that hope was for fools."

"Well!" said Ruthie indignantly, her cheeks bright and her eyes snappy. "If you ask me, I think Uncle Hendrick is foolish *and* hopeless."

Snow was falling thick and fast. Enough had accumulated on the ground that the children kicked up cascades of it as they walked.

"Let's hurry," said Stirling. "It's getting slippery."

"I bet they'll have to call off school tomorrow," said Ruthie joyfully.

"Hurray!" cheered Kit and Stirling. "No school!" After that, the children didn't talk much. It was too hard to talk, because the wind was blowing the snow into their faces. Kit pulled her hat down over her ears and held her collar closed over her mouth. She bent forward, her shoulders hunched. The wind seemed to be coming from every direction at once. Sometimes it pushed against Kit as if trying to stop her. Then suddenly it would swoop around and push her from behind as if it were trying to hasten her along.

Kit thought it was a very good thing that she and Ruthie and Stirling knew the way to River Street so well. They had to walk with their eyes squinted shut against the stinging snow. Slowly they made their way to the alley behind the soup kitchen and up to its back door. They stopped to stomp the snow off their boots before they opened the door and went inside. The cooking area was busier than ever. And when the three children pushed through the big swinging door, they saw that the front room where the food was served was terribly crowded because of the harsh, wet weather.

"Oh, my," whispered Kit in dismay. The room smelled of wet wool. It seemed to Kit to be awash in a sea of gray, filled as it was with people wearing their snow-soaked winter coats and hats.

"I think," said Ruthie firmly, "we should give my old coats and shoes to someone in charge. I don't see how we'd choose who needs them most."

Kit agreed. The hobo children's coats and shoes were even worse than she remembered. They were so worn-out and filthy! They were such pitiful protection against the cold and wet of a day like today.

Stirling asked a woman serving food, and she pointed out the director of the soup kitchen. It took the three children a while to wriggle their way through the crowd to her. The room was so packed, it was hard not to jostle anyone or step on anyone's feet.

When they finally reached the director, Ruthie said, "Excuse me, ma'am. We brought these coats and shoes. We were hoping you'd give them to some children who need them."

"Why, thank you," said the director as she took the things from Ruthie. "I'll have no trouble finding new owners for these." She sighed. "Not many people think of the children. We have more and more children passing through here now, and all are in such desperate need."

After the director spoke, Kit remembered her own voice saying to Uncle Hendrick, "*If people knew about the hobo children . . .*" Kit slid her hand into her pocket to be sure her letter to the newspaper about the hobo children was safe. As she did, she felt something hard in her pocket. It was her camera. Again, she heard her own voice. This time it was saying, "*If they saw how terrible the children's coats and shoes are, I'm sure they'd help.*"

Kit had an idea. Eagerly, she took her camera out of her pocket. "Would it be all right if we took some photographs of the children?" she asked the director.

"You must ask the children's permission and their parents', too," answered the director. "If they say yes, it's all right with me."

"Thanks!" said Kit. She and Ruthie and Stirling shared a quick grin. Kit did not even have to explain her brainstorm to her friends. They figured it out right away.

"We'll put the film in the envelope with your letter," said Ruthie.

"As I always say, a picture tells more about a person than words ever could," said Stirling.

Then they went into action. It was quite remarkable, Kit thought, how well they worked as a team. Without even talking about it, each one took a separate job. Ruthie asked the children if they'd like to have their pictures taken and explained politely to the parents what Kit wanted to do. Stirling told the children where to sit or stand and arranged their coats so that they'd show up clearly in the picture.

Kit worked the camera. She didn't have a flash, so she had to use light from the window. First she took pictures that showed the children from head to toe. Then she took pictures of the children's feet and makeshift shoes. Some children had taken their shoes off and lined them up to dry by a hissing radiator. Kit took a picture of the sad parade of shoes, which looked as exhausted as the children to whom they belonged. None of the shoes looked as if they could go another step.

Too soon, Kit had used all her film. "That's it,"

she said to Ruthie and Stirling. She put the film in the envelope with her letter. "Let's go."

The snowstorm was cruel and furious now. As Kit led Ruthie and Stirling to the newspaper offices, the children were blown and buffeted by the ice-cold wind. Every inch of the way was hard-won. It was a great relief to go inside the big brick building and be out of the swirling snow. It was very warm inside. Snow melted off the children's coats and boots and left a wet trail behind them as they climbed the stairs and walked through the newsroom to Gibb's desk.

Kit took the two letters out of her pocket, then hesitated. *Plip, plop.* The snow melting off her coat made an apologetic sound as it dripped to the floor. A small puddle formed around Kit's feet. Drops from her hat hit the letters.

"Put it in the box," ordered Gibb with even more impatience and less enthusiasm than usual. As always, he did not bother to look up.

Kit took a deep breath. She put the letter from Uncle Hendrick in the in-box. Under it she slid her own letter, which was bulgy with the roll of film and rather damp and wrinkled.

The three children left the newsroom and walked down the stairs. "Do you suppose they'll use the photos we took?" asked Stirling as the children paused to prepare themselves to face the storm before they went out of the newspaper office building.

"I don't know," Kit said.

"I wonder if they'll print your letter," mused Ruthie as she pulled on her mittens. "And if they do print it, do you think it'll change anything?"

"I don't know that, either," said Kit. She grinned crookedly. "Don't tell Uncle Hendrick, but I *hope* so."

The world was quiet, clean, and innocent under its fresh white layer of snow the next morning when Kit went out to walk Inky and buy Uncle Hendrick's newspaper. Uncle Hendrick always pitched a fit if his newspaper had been unfolded and read before he got it. So, even though she was bursting with curiosity, Kit knew she must not open up the paper to see if her letter and the photos had been printed. She had pretty much convinced herself that Gibb had tossed them in the trash. Still, it was hard not to feel optimistic on a beautiful morning like this, with the sun making a sparkling prism of every flake that caught its reflection.

Kit delivered the newspaper, his breakfast tray, and Inky to Uncle Hendrick. She fiddled awhile undoing the leash from Inky's collar, hoping that Uncle Hendrick would open up the newspaper and turn to the editorial page. But instead, Uncle Hendrick turned to her and said, "I don't want you now." So Kit had to leave.

She went downstairs and helped Mother serve breakfast to the boarders. They were all seated at the table when suddenly they heard Uncle Hendrick bellow and Inky yowl. Kit jumped up to go see what was the matter. But before she took a step, Uncle Hendrick exploded out of his room and came clomping down the stairs, with Inky yip-yapping close behind him. "What's the meaning of this?" Uncle Hendrick shouted, waving the newspaper over his head.

Kit sat down hard. *Could it be?* she wondered.

"Hello, Uncle Hendrick," said Mother, trying to calm him. "We are so pleased to see you back on your feet again!"

"Never mind," growled Uncle Hendrick. He slapped the newspaper onto the table, setting all the china rattling and making the silverware clink. Ignoring everyone else, he glared at Kit. "What have you done, young lady?"

Kit kicked Stirling under the table. They both tried to hide their smiles.

"I might have known you were in on it, too," Uncle Hendrick said to Stirling. "Young whippersnapper!"

"What is going on?" asked Dad. He picked up the newspaper and exclaimed, "Well, for heaven's sakes! There's a letter to the editor here from Kit. And there are photos with it, too!"

Pandemonium broke loose. Everyone jumped up from the table, all talking at once, and crowded around Dad to get a look at the newspaper. They didn't pay any attention to Uncle Hendrick, who was standing in the background making an angry speech to no one, pounding the floor with his cane, his remarks punctuated by Inky's barks. Grace, who loved mayhem, added her hoarse woofs to the hubbub, too.

"Settle down!" Dad called out. When everyone

was quiet, even Uncle Hendrick and Inky, Dad said, "I'm going to read Kit's letter aloud. I want everyone to listen."

Kit felt a warm blush begin at her toes and climb all the way up to the top of her head as Dad read her letter. Mother came and stood behind Kit's chair and put her hands on Kit's shoulders. When Dad had finished reading, she said, "Kit, I'm proud of you!" She leaned down and kissed Kit's cheek.

This was too much for Uncle Hendrick. "Proud?" he said, aghast. "Proud of that impudent girl?" He pointed an angry finger at Kit. "And you, a mere child, writing a letter to the newspaper! Where did you get such an idea?"

"Why, from you, of course, Uncle Hendrick," answered Kit politely.

Uncle Hendrick was speechless. A strange expression crossed his face. It seemed to be a mixture of annoyance and something that could have been respect. It lasted only a moment. Then Uncle Hendrick turned away and stalked off, Inky trailing behind him.

After that, everyone congratulated Kit, and Stirling, too. But Kit barely heard them. She held

the newspaper in her two hands and looked at her letter and the photographs. Thousands of people would read this newspaper and see the photos. Thousands of people would read words that *she* had written. Kit shivered with delight. She could hardly believe it was true.

Ruthie was right. School *was* closed that day because of the snow. In fact, school was closed for a week after the storm, which turned out to have been the worst blizzard to hit Cincinnati in years.

So it was more than a week later, at the end of the first day back, that Kit, Ruthie, and Stirling found themselves walking to the soup kitchen after school. Lots of Kit's classmates had read her letter and seen the photos in the newspaper. They had brought their old coats and shoes to school. Some of Kit and Stirling's egg customers had also seen the letter and the photos, and they had made donations of clothing, too. Kit and Stirling were staggering under armloads of coats, and Ruthie was pulling the wagon, which was full of boots and shoes. They

*Thousands of people would read words that **she** had written. Kit shivered with delight. She could hardly believe it was true.*

brought their donations straight to the director of the soup kitchen.

The director smiled broadly at them. "I am so glad to see the three of you!" she said. "You're the children who took the photos, aren't you?"

Kit, Ruthie, and Stirling nodded.

The director asked Kit, "And are you the one who wrote the letter?"

"Yes, ma'am," said Kit.

"We've had many more donations for the children since your letter and those photos appeared in the newspaper," said the director. "You drew attention to a real need. You three have truly made a difference. Thank you."

"You're welcome," said Kit, Ruthie, and Stirling, beaming.

As it happened, Kit had another letter of Uncle Hendrick's to deliver to the newspaper office. This one was about Eleanor Roosevelt. Uncle Hendrick highly disapproved of the work she was doing to help miners in West Virginia. The letter was so full of fiery words that Kit was surprised it wasn't hot to the touch.

This time, it was a quick, easy walk to the newspaper building, since the weather was clear. Upstairs, the newsroom was just as noisy and busy as ever, and Gibb was as distracted as always when the children came to his desk. Kit started to put Uncle Hendrick's letter in Gibb's in-box.

"Hold on," said Gibb.

Kit stopped.

Gibb tilted his head toward the letter. "Is that one of his or one of yours?" he asked.

"His," Kit answered.

"Put it in the box," said Gibb in his usual brusque way. Then his voice changed. "But any time you've got something else *you* want to write, bring it here. You've got the makings of a good reporter, kid."

Kit was so happy she could hardly speak. "Thanks," she said. Out of the corner of her eye, she saw Ruthie and Stirling nudge each other and grin.

The three of them walked home together along the slushy sidewalks, dodging puddles of melted snow. But the sky was blue overhead, and there was a certain softness in the air that seemed to Kit to carry the scent of spring. It was just a hint, just a whiff, but it was full of promise.

That's it, thought Kit. *That's the perfect word. I feel full of **promise**.*

Looking
Back
1934

A PEEK INTO
THE PAST

Waiting for job interviews at an employment agency

Kit's story ends in 1934, but the Great Depression continued until the early 1940s. By 1934, many American families were in the same position as the Kittredges. They had found ways to make ends meet in spite of lost jobs and lost hopes, but times were still hard and they had no idea when the Depression might end. Everyone did whatever was necessary to survive and hoped that the newly elected president could find a way to end the Depression.

These girls helped their school save money by cleaning up the school themselves.

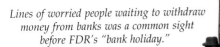

Lines of worried people waiting to withdraw money from banks was a common sight before FDR's "bank holiday."

President Franklin Delano Roosevelt knew he needed to act fast to fight the Depression. One of the first official acts during his first one hundred days in office dealt with the banks. By 1933, thousands of banks had run out of money and closed, taking many people's life savings with them. People got scared when they heard about bank closings. They rushed to take all their money out of their local banks, which created even more problems—and sometimes caused banks to fail completely.

To stop more banks from failing, Roosevelt declared a "bank holiday" and temporarily closed all banks. He then went on the radio and told the public exactly what he was doing. He explained to people that their money would be safe because the government would *insure* their accounts. Under his new plan, if a bank failed and couldn't pay its customers, the government promised to step in and make sure the depositors got their money back. Americans were reassured by Roosevelt's words, and took their money back to the banks.

Roosevelt's radio address about America's banks was the first of many radio "fireside chats" broadcast to the American people.

Along with bold action to stabilize the banks, President Roosevelt created relief and jobs programs as part of the "new deal" he had promised Americans during the election. With the help of business leaders, Roosevelt and the National Recovery Administration (NRA) set minimum wages and maximum hours for workers, so workers earned a higher hourly wage and jobs could be spread among as many workers as possible. People were encouraged to buy products made under the NRA, and the NRA blue eagle began to be used as a show of support for the program.

Some New Deal programs didn't last long. The Civil Works Administration (CWA) created part-time jobs for older men, such as Kit's dad, but it lasted only a few months.

These Hollywood starlets showed their support by having the NRA eagle suntanned on their backs!

WPA artists worked on projects ranging from huge painted murals to posters to hand-carved puppets.

The Works Progress Administration (WPA) replaced the CWA in early 1935, and it *was* successful. Public buildings still in use today were built under this program, and many included murals and art created by WPA artists. Other programs, such as the Federal Writers' Project, the Federal Music Program, and the Federal Theater Project, provided jobs to writers, musicians, and actors.

One of Roosevelt's most enduring New Deal programs—and one still in effect today—was the Social Security Administration. It provided for and protected retirement funds for American workers.

The first Social Security cards were issued in December 1936.

WHAT DID YOU SAY YOUR NAME IS?

723-411-606

Social Security assigned a number to all workers in order to keep track of their retirement funds, but some people didn't like being identified by a number.

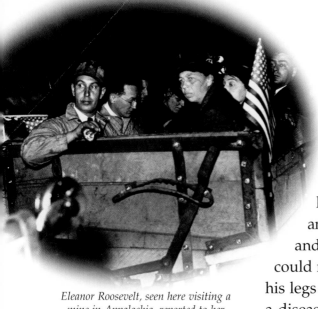

Eleanor Roosevelt, seen here visiting a mine in Appalachia, reported to her husband everything she saw in her travels.

Eleanor Roosevelt was one of the most active First Ladies ever. She considered herself to be the eyes and ears of the President, and she went places he could not easily go, because his legs were paralyzed by a disease called *polio*. Many Americans, grateful for her public presence and her concern for people in need, grew to respect and love Mrs. Roosevelt.

However, like Kit's Uncle Hendrick, other Americans detested both Franklin and Eleanor Roosevelt. People like Uncle Hendrick believed that the New Deal programs were bad for America and did not like what they thought of as government "meddling" in business and in private citizens' lives.

In spite of the Roosevelts' efforts, the Depression continued through the 1930s. Things improved slightly—and slowly—as America tried to climb out of the slippery hole of the Depression. Temporary jobs were created, but when funds

Children suffered from hunger lack of adequate clothing when parents didn't have jobs.

Dust storms blew huge clouds of dust and dirt across the Midwest and the South.

ran out and unemployment rose again in a *recession*, the country's economy started slipping back into the hole of the Depression. During the 1937 recession, FDR reported grimly, "I see one-third of a nation ill-housed, ill-clad, ill-nourished," as he continued to search for solutions to America's problems.

Among the lowest points were the great dust storms in the Midwest. Careless farming practices and prolonged *drought,* or dry spells, caused rich topsoil to dry up and blow away in huge gray and brown clouds. Hundreds of thousands of families lost their farms and went west to California, where they did temporary farmwork and lived under miserable conditions in migrant camps.

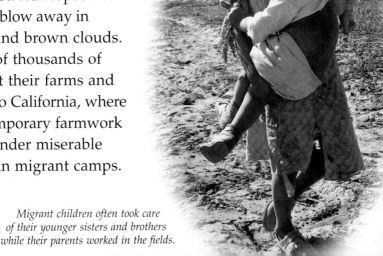

Migrant children often took care of their younger sisters and brothers while their parents worked in the fields.

The Depression finally ended, in part because of another crisis, one that had been brewing overseas for years. In the 1920s and 1930s, a German leader named Adolf Hitler had been gaining power. Germany had suffered its own depression after losing World War One in 1918, and Hitler promised the German people a return to prosperity if they followed him.

Adolf Hitler salutes his followers, wh *were known as **Nazis**.*

Hitler also rebuilt the German army and started invading other European countries. He formed partnerships with Italy in Europe and with Japan in the Pacific. In addition, Hitler *persecuted* certain groups, or treated them harshly and unfairly. Among those groups were Jewish people, Gypsies, Jehovah's Witnesses, and others whose politics and lifestyles he did not agree with. Americans were concerned about Hitler's increasing power, but most did not want to fight in another war overseas. Instead, America helped its *allies*, its friends who were fighting Germany, by producing war supplies.

Factories geared up to produce war goods to fight Germany.

Japanese pilots took this photo of their attack on the U.S. Army base next to Pearl Harbor. After the attack, America declared war.

The new factory jobs created to produce war supplies for America's allies helped end the Depression in the United States. Americans were happy to have a growing economy again, but most still did not want to go to war. However, in December 1941, Japan attacked the United States by bombing the Hawaiian port of Pearl Harbor, and America entered the war.

Kit would have been 18 years old when America entered World War Two. She might have become a nurse or a factory worker. Or, with her talent for writing, Kit

A World War Two war correspondent

might have become a war correspondent, covering the war and writing stories about what she saw. The same resourcefulness, hard work, cooperation, and compassion that got Kit and other Americans through the Depression were what they relied on to get through the war years. By the time the Great Depression and World War Two ended, Americans were ready for peace, prosperity, and stability.

At the war's end, families gathered to celebrate peace and the return to prosperity.

An Honest Answer

by Ginger Andrews

Ginger Andrews

WINNER OF THE 12TH ANNUAL

NICHOLAS ROERICH POETRY PRIZE
STORY LINE PRESS
1999

Published by Story Line Press, Inc.
Three Oaks Farm
PO Box 1240
Ashland, OR 97520-0055

This publication was made possible thanks in part to the generous support of the
Nicholas Roerich Museum, the Andrew W. Mellon Foundation, the National
Endowment for the Arts, and our individual contributors.

Book design by Lysa McDowell

Library of Congress Cataloging-in-Publication Data

Andrews, Ginger, 1956–
        An honest answer / by Ginger Andrews.
          p.   cm.
        ISBN 1-885266-78-2 (alk. paper)
        1. Working class—United States Poetry. I. Title.
        PS3551.N4177H6 1999
        811'.54—dc21

Acknowledgements
Grateful acknowledgement is made to the editors of the following journals in
which some of thes poems or earlier versions of them first appeared.

The Beacon: "My Sister Calls" and "Growing Old Near Charleston"
Fireweed: "Rolls-Royce Dreams, " "Prayer," "Old Bawling Hags," "Habitual
Offender," "Going Down" and "O That Summer"
The Hudson Review: "An Early Spring," "The Day I looked In the Mirror and
Saw Nothing," "Mikey Likes It" and "Thanksgiving"
The New Press: "A Place Prepared"
Poetry: "With A Wicked Little Jab," "No Code" and "Not Sleeping Too Good
Myself"
RiverSedge: "Friday Night," "Sister Ritual" and "This Poem"
The Writer: "The Housewife" (under the title "Out Any Bedroom Window")

Special thanks to The Coos Bay Writers Workshop and Lowell Jaeger who chose
the poem "Thanksgiving" as the 1997 winner of the Mary Scheirman Poetry
Award. Ongoing thanks to "Catfish" Dave, Josephine Bridges, Mikey, the Tuesday night critique group, and Marilyn Nelson who said, "Only believe."

For Mary Beth

CONTENTS

PART THREE:
WHAT THE CLEANING LADY KNOWS

PART FOUR:
NOT SLEEPING TOO GOOD MYSELF

*A prearranged agreement for no life support.

"An honest answer is like a kiss on the lips." —Proverbs 24:26

In memory
Frank Dearstine
Francis Almeda Dearstine
Tana Rae Dooley

A Whole Life

The presiding spirit behind Ginger Andrews' first book *An Honest Answer* must be William Carlos Williams. When he said he wrote in the speech of Polish mothers, he could have included the American working class anywhere. The sinewy resilience of Andrews' individual poems honors the tradition of his free verse lyrics. She listens for the poetic measure in American speech and reproduces it in unique forms. I would venture to say that the poetry of Ginger Andrews is as close to the tradition of Williams as American free verse has ever been.

Where Andrews' poems seem fragmentary at times, like those poems of Williams which Robert Frost called "snippets of things," they are in fact parts that stand for a whole, as Frost himself said any poem was—a part that stood for a whole. In Andrews' case each part stands for a whole life. That life in An Honest Answer follows a narrative arc: the early death of her mother, the illness and eventual death of her father, and the effect of these losses on herself and her surviving siblings. The operative word here is survivor. That word, used loosely twenty years ago about upwardly mobile young people, applies to Andrews: she's a survivor, saved, apparently, by her faith and her poetry. She is never just marking time, never boring, never setting herself a mere exercise. She is acknowledged among her family and friends as their poet, recorder of life and hard times in the lumber towns of the Northwest, where astounding natural beauty is no remedy for the grim facts of joblessness, alcoholism, crime, disease. Andrews shows how poetry breaks through the dank fog of these troubles, as surely as her profound and durable faith.

As for the voice speaking to us in these poems, it is as fresh as Ray Carver's seemed 25 years ago. Another poet who comes to mind is her fellow Northwesterner Vern Rutsala, himself a descendent of Williams who, like Williams, has kept his eye on the working poor throughout his career. Andrews is a working class, born again Sappho, an Ahkmatova who cleans houses and teaches Sunday School. These figures come to mind not for the sake of hyperbole, but to help understand the originality of this new and remarkable poet. We glimpse one vital source of her imagination in the opening of "Home Alone":

> Cigarette smokers,
> sweet tooths,
> alcoholics, teetotalers,
> bad cooks, good cooks,
> food stamp recipients,
> low blood sugar & type 2 diabetes,
> depression, codependency, cancer,
> high energy, low self-esteem,
> nap takers, neat freaks, control freaks,
> carpal tunnel syndrome,
> strong arms, skinny ankles, pot bellies,
> public speakers, introverts, braggers,
> blue eyes, long legs, red necks,
> enablers, naggers, whiners,
> pride, guilt and honesty all run in my family.

And she adds, "There's never a dull moment, though I'm praying for one." Ginger Andrews speaks to us genuinely and passionately from firsthand experience, and in doing so, she speaks for others who share that experience and share it every day.

— Mark Jarman

PART ONE:
ROLLS-ROYCE DREAMS

The Day I Looked In The Mirror
And Saw Nothing

It was late afternoon. Ninety-plus degrees in Dillard, Oregon.
Dad was pulling green chain at Hult Lumber Company.
I'd been missing Mom real bad, but remembered her last days
Of pain, how cancer made her cry out, and I knew
There was no pain in heaven.
My three oldest sisters were married and gone.
My sweet, habitual offender brother was doing time
For some stupid parole violation.
There was just my sister Mary Beth and me at home.
She was playing Credence Clearwater Revival's *Proud Mary*
On our cheap stereo.
I was wondering what we'd cook for dinner
Besides canned soup. And I was wondering,
Being thirteen and all, if I'd ever get any breasts.
My older sisters wore 34B, C, or *D*.
I thought I'd just lock myself in the bathroom
And check to see if maybe
I'd grown a little bit.

ReClassified

WW II took just about any man,
but Dad couldn't see too good
out of one eye, was blind in the other,
had high blood pressure,
three kids and a wife.

They bused him
from Jefferson Barracks in Saint Louis
back home to Gideon
where he worked at a box factory
making just enough money to feed his family
and keep a roof over our heads,

and where some folks called him
a 4-F son of a bitch.

First Love

In sixth grade
there was a boy I liked.
He liked me too. I could tell.

His mother was room-mother
at our school parties.
I was jealous
because she was pretty,
brought fancy store-bought treats,
and because my mom had to go to heaven
the summer before I started fourth grade.

He lived four streets up from me
in a beautiful house
with a trimmed hedge
and a painted gold picket fence.

I lived in an ugly house
(I hoped he'd never see)
with faded gray siding
and grass that needed mowed.

Playing tag with my sister
in our front yard one day after school,
I saw him across the street
at the neighbor boy's house.

I waved and said *Hi*.
He said *Hi*.

But he didn't wave back.

I went inside and watched him
till he rode off
on his shiny new red bike.

The next day at school
he was friendly,
but not as friendly as before.
And that's my first love story.
There's nothing more to tell.

Milk Cow Blues

I never once saw Dad kiss Momma.
Never even saw him hold her hand. But
he sang her a song about a milk cow,
how he was havin' to go without both milk and butter
ever since his milk cow'd been gone:

> *If you see my milk cow,*
> *pleeeease send her on home to me.*
> *I ain't had no milk or butterrrrr*
> *since my milk coooow's been gone.*

Sometimes he sang the song over and over.
His voice would crack flat
when he tried hitting the high notes.
Momma's shoulders would shake.
She'd tuck her chin to her chest, reaching
to wipe tears from her eyes with the corner of her apron.
It had to be
some kind of love.

Rolls-Royce Dreams

Using salal leaves for money,
my youngest sister and I
paid an older sister
to taxi an abandoned car
in our backyard. Our sister
knew how to shift gears,
turn smoothly with a hand signal,
and make perfect screeching stop sounds.

We drove to the beach,
to the market, to Sunday School,
past our would-be boyfriends' houses,
to any town, anywhere.
We shopped for expensive clothes everywhere.
Our sister would open our doors
and say, *Meter's runnin' ladies,*
but take your time.

We rode all over in that ugly green Hudson
with its broken front windshield, springs poking
through its back seat, blackberry vines growing
through rusted floorboards;
with no wheels, no tires, taillights busted,
headlights missing, and gas gauge on empty.

Love Poem For My Brother

You were so cool,
so handsome in a white T-shirt,
penny loafers and tight jeans,
driving that beat up Ford
with reversed shackles.
I gave you the big green stuffed snake
I'd won at the school carnival
to put in the rear window dash.
You told me I was a good girl.

I remember Momma crying
when Dad beat you with a garden hose
after you broke in Barview store
for beer and cigarettes,
when you went to Maclaren School for Boys,
and when you did time at the Oregon State Pen
for something statutory. Everybody said
she lied. I'm sorry you were up there
when Momma died.

Blessed Gospel Light

A full-bore black-out alcoholic
from the time she drank her first beer,
she lost a lot of good years,
passed by marriage proposals
from good-looking men
in three-piece suits
with cars and houses
already paid for, to marry
a no-'count demented drunk
who swore his favorite song
was *How Great Thou Art*
with one hand on his heart,
the other tucked inside the top
of his too-tight button-fly 501 blues.

She worked her way up
scrubbing floors, making beds,
waiting tables, tending bar,
to hit rock bottom one cold night —
beaten half to death by small town cops
in a big city way.

Reading AA's big blue book
with one eye — the other swollen shut —
lying stiff, broken, blood and beer-stained

on a jail cell bed, she cried
while quietly praying out loud
to the heavenly higher power.

A Sunday School teacher now —
she traded in her booze for a Bible,
honky tonk days for the Better Way,
the Truth, the Life.
There's a Glory that shines about her.
Ask her, and she'll tell you:
It's the good Lord shining,
it's the Blessed Gospel Light.

December Morning

Drinking Chase & Sanborn
from unmatched cups
without saucers
on a cold December morning
at my sister's place
on her first day off in quite some time,
we talk

about growing up poor
but happy as ticks,
how we still ain't got much,
but we don't care.

So we both dropped out of school.
I got married & had babies.
She got drunk & stayed drunk about eight years.
We add up broken dreams & hearts
and my sister wins.

We pretend we're sipping
General Foods International Coffee —
Café Francais. I tell her
Jean-Luc thought I was cute,
but thought she was the prettiest
thing he'd ever seen.

And we talk
about how she doesn't drink anymore,
and me, finally going back to school.

We raise our coffee cups
and clink them together across the table,
little fingers held high.

Don't Know Much About Algebra

All through grade school
I thought if I was *really* smart,
everybody would love me.
I had to fake it in math.
By the time high school rolled around,
in order to keep up appearances, I signed up for algebra.
About two weeks later, I snapped, admitted to the teacher
and whoever else cared, that I didn't get it.
There was this blue-eyed senior jock who played drums
and had an eye for me. We ran off and got married.
I got pregnant on my honeymoon night in a cheap motel
    in Reno,
had morning sickness, dry heaves, for two solid months.
It was nice though, I told myself, to be out of my dad's shack,
where the toilet never flushed and the place always smelled
like Salem cigarettes.

The Housewife

sits on her carefully made bed.
Her blue curtains are more than half drawn.
All household members are acting perfectly rational.
So everyone is a little boring.
So everyone is a little crazy.
She could pick up
her somewhat expensive marble-based candelabra —
and throw it out her window
because she's bored,
because she's just a little crazy.
For any one of a hundred reasons,
she could throw it.
But she won't.
She'll straighten the bed covers
and, maybe, later,
she'll burn the hell out of dinner.

Come To Papa

Sitting in a rusty-armed lawn chair
in Dad's overgrown backyard, worried sick
over what direction my life might take. Afraid
to burden this dying man, afraid he'll tell me
I've made my bed and I'll have to lie in it, or preach
about how folks with good common sense know better
than to jump out of a fire and into a frying pan.

We sit quietly till he looks me straight in the eye, slowly
crosses one skeleton-thin leg over the other, and says, hell
is being old, sick and alone. He offers the other half of an apple
he just can't eat. But Dad, I say, it's rotten.
> *For chrissake kid, cut out the bad part.*
> *If you had the brains of a peckerwood*
> *I swear you'd fly backwards. Just because*
> *you have shit running down one drawer-leg*
> *doesn't mean it's running down the other.*

Divorce Poem

You got the house
with double car garage,
work bench and tools

the kitchen
with solid oak cabinets,
built-in stove, dishwasher
and garbage disposal

one and three-quarter baths
with heat lamps, fans,
and full length mirrors

the music room
with stereo, AM / FM
tuner, equalizer,
Infinity speakers,
keyboard, microphones,
all the records,
all the tapes,
and the ten-piece
top-of-the-line
Rogers double-bass drum kit

the family room
with custom-made drapes
and the floor-to-ceiling
solid-rock fireplace
half the furniture,
half the linen,
half the dishes
half the pictures on the walls

the thirty-five millimeter
camera with telephoto lens
and tripod

the 5.6 acres,
water rights to the creek,
the grass, the trees,
the flowers
and the dog

the lawn mower
and the rototiller

the blue Chevy
short-bed pickup truck
and my ex-best friend.

I got both our boys.

PART TWO:
O THAT SUMMER

Before Our Divorces

when my sister was tending bar weekends,
drinking, or snorting a line most days, she'd call
knowing my husband was at work,
that he didn't like her, and couldn't understand
why I loved her like crazy. He thought
we were complete opposites, and I agreed,
being a Sunday School teacher and all.

After our divorces
when she'd stopped drinking and I was considering it
and a possible affair, though I couldn't imagine
who would want me, she'd call or drop by
to water my plants, tell me I was crazy,
ask if I was going to church Sunday,
did I have an extra pair of panty hose, a dress,
and a dadgum freaking pair of heels
that she maybe could borrow.

I Tell Them I'm A Bible School Teacher

I tell my old friends that I'm a housewife / homemaker,
still a small town girl. Finally got out of Charleston,
never dreaming I'd be back.

>   *... Say you're about, what, thirty-four,*
>   *thirty-five now?*

I tell them that I was married at sixteen
for twelve, almost thirteen years. Divorced.
Remarried about four years ago now.

>   *So you married another Mike? —*
>   *The one from Barview — Tarheel Road —*
>   *that Mike? Well how 'bout that.*

I say my oldest sister's still here,
in North Bend now. She's the mayor's wife.
I say Mary Beth's a recovering alcoholic,
that she's still the prettiest one,
that she still tells me what to do.

>   *Is your Dad still around?*
>   *What about your other sisters?*
>   *And where in the hell is your brother now anyway...?*

I tell them I'm a Bible school teacher
at the North Bend Church of Christ.

But I don't tell them
how the kids in my class
love to march in the infantry,
or how beautiful their little voices sound
when they sing "Jesus Loves Me" off-key.
I don't say
that they too could hear them sing
if they happen to pass by Broadway Street
on any Wednesday night.

And I say I'm crazy
not to tell them that.

On Certain Sunny Sundays

On the way to K-Mart
after church services,
we pass by a tight-bunned,
blue-eyed, hairy chested
construction worker .
and start talking dirty
(like only two sisters can)
and we laugh and laugh
almost going off the road
and my sister says that we are so bad
even God doesn't know
what to do with us —
and what a scary thought that is.
But we laugh and laugh
until we cry and cry
because we're getting older
and aren't nearly as pretty
as we used to be
and because we act so stupid and silly,
struggle with our teenagers,
jobs, periods and prayers.
And we cry
because we love each other
like only two sisters can
after church services
on the way to K-Mart
on certain sunny Sundays.

Friday Night

My oldest son called.
He's working full-time,
got his own place now
and taking some night classes at UCC.

At 9:30 my sixteen-year-old son
(they tell me he's an angel)
kissed my cheek goodnight.

You bought me my favorite perfume
on Mother's Day.

Dinner's dishes are washed
and put away.

The house is clean.

All our bills are paid.

                If I drank

I guess I'd go get drunk.

O That Summer

my sister and I
both wound up back in Coos Bay,
basket cases, lonely as hell.
She was recovering from drugs and alcohol,
I was newly divorced, a Sunday School teacher
with no job skills whatsoever
and two little boys to feed,
praying for a maid job at Best Western.
Lord how we prayed

walking from one end
of Sunset Beach to the other, barefoot,
freezing in tank tops and cutoffs,
hair and makeup perfect,
fingernails painted with three coats
of Wet'n Wild, hoping
some good looking single doctor
was walking his dog nearby
should one of us happen
to slice our foot on beach glass.

Evidently, She Says,

she's looking for a man physically
and / or mentally abused as a child.
He has a sad but sexy smile,
long eyelashes,
and wears Levis exclusively.
He works hard
when he works.
He draws maximum unemployment benefits
whenever he's laid off. He has been
married two or three times, is currently
behind on his child support payments
but should be back working any day,
plans to get caught up,
is good in bed,
smokes pot, drinks beer, does drugs,
presently has no transportation,
and is obviously in need of a good home-
cooked meal.
She's looking, she says,
for a sick man.
The sicker, the better.

Cruising The Slammer

I am talking LOW self-esteem, this pretty woman says,
at one point I'd call up a man, invite him over knowing
the only thing I could count on from the long-legged
    good-looking jerk
was a lay.
Oh Honey, this other gal says, I used to cruise
the county jail with my girlfriend. She'd toot her horn
to get the guys' attention through the barred windows.
When they'd wave back I was sooooo thrilled!
But, hey, my friend was worse off than me,
she actually wrote them letters.

Prayer

God bless the chick in Alaska
who took in my sister's ex,
an abusive alcoholic hunk.
Bless all borderline brainless ex-cheerleaders
with long blonde hair, boobs,
and waists no bigger around than a coke bottle
who've broken up somebody else's home.
Forgive my thrill
should they put on seventy-five pounds,
develop stretch marks, spider veins,
and suffer through endless days of deep depression.

Bless those who remarry on the rebound.
Bless me and all my sisters;
the ball and chain baggage
we carried into our second marriages.
Bless my broken brother and his live-in.
Grant him SSI. Consider
how the deeper the wounds in my family,
the funnier we've become.
Bless those who've learned to laugh at what's longed for.
Keep us from becoming hilarious.
Bless our children.
Bless all our ex's,
and bless the fat chick in Alaska.

Necessity

You need to live
near the edge of the world
on Broadway Street in my small port town.

You need sweet neighbors
who grow pale pink fuchsias under Plexiglas,
and bright red and yellow dahlias — right up through
    gravel.

You need four sisters
who are as kind hearted as mine,
and think every poem you write is perfect.

You need an alcoholic brother
who's seen the inside of hard time,
whose blue eyes look just like yours.

You need a mother who died young,
a mother who cooked the best plain brown beans in the
    whole world,
a mother who taught you to share, made you feel rich
though you were poor.

You need a mother
who showed you where wild tiger lilies grow,
a mother who dressed you and your sisters
as pretty as she could for Jesus.

You need a foulmouthed old fart for a father —
who makes you laugh.

You need my dunes, my trees, my ocean,
my fog and routine rain.

You need my modest, middle-class income home.

You need my trusty, rusting '84 Ford
whose odometer reads one-hundred
and twenty-six thousand miles.

You need my $7.50 an hour house cleaning jobs,
Tuesdays through Fridays.
You need to pull weeds and trim your laurel hedge.

You need to live on the edge of the world
and, oh, how you need Jesus.

My Sister Calls

to say she's lost weight
and her old jeans fit again.
She says it's kinda neat
having her whole system screwed up
from falling out of love,
that it's not much different
than falling *in* love,
not that she's in any hurry.

Her check garnishment ends
on the 21st, and would I like to go
to garage sales with her that weekend?
She's got an antique dealer coming
sometime this morning
to buy her dark wood dresser
with the mirror. She's afraid
she'll let it go
for far less than what it's worth
but she didn't really call to complain,
she wants to know
if I've written any good poems lately
and I tell her I'm writing
just as fast as I can.

A Place Prepared

It's such a sad world.
Don't we all get on with it though?
I, for example, am upset
because I've lost a shoe
and am tearing up
an almost clean house to find it
so I can run to the store for carrots.
I have everything else I need
for a chuck roast dinner,
went to the store last night
and bought half a dozen
unnecessary things, but forgot my carrots.
Can you believe it?

I've got a sister
saving up money she doesn't have
for a divorce she doesn't want,
another sister praying
'cause she's been there. My dad's feet
are turning black from diabetes,
and about half the people I know
are recovering from an addiction.
The other half are in denial.

I've been trying to read
three chapters from the gospels every day.
I'm twenty-seven chapters behind.

But I believe
that all my poems are prayers,
that it's OK to ask God for anything, anytime;
that it's OK to sit down
in the middle of your floor and cry
because you've lost a shoe,
that it's OK to ask Him
for a glimpse
of what it will feel like
stepping into that place
He's promised to prepare.

Way Past Dancing

It doesn't bother him that he can't get it up anymore.
Old age and diabetes will slow a man way down, and besides,
Sex is for young folks, and Lord knows he had his share.
Never had any complaints either. Getting women was easy
If you were the only guy for miles with a Model A Ford,
And, if you knew how to dance.

His legs are numb, his feet are swollen.
Imagine, he says, *having to sit to piss.*

Swatting flies on the back porch, I ask, *Dad, are you hungry?*
He pops out his upper teeth, shows me where they broke
Night before last when he was trying to eat peanuts,
How he's fixed them good as new with Crazy glue.

An Early Spring

We've all been devastated
since week before last
when my husband's best buddy took his own life.
Thirty-eight years old. He wasn't even drunk..
We can't imagine what we'll do with his mother.
We're just sick

about the earthquake in Japan, tired of O.J., cold rain
and Jehovah's Witnesses knocking
asking questions like, are you suffering from burnout?

This last divorce has all but done my sister in.
Her big old red Ford sits broken down
under our carport, finally out of the rain.
Mushrooms grow on its back floorboard.
My sister plans to stay just till she's back on her feet.
Her five-year-old spoiled brat of a kid
calls me Grumpy Old Aunt Gin,
tells me she misses her Daddy
and that she's scared bad of her Uncle Mikey
'cause he makes her mind.
She's into my underwear, my makeup—
I can't find my blush anywhere.
She asks endless questions like, does Jesus have a girlfriend?
Today she handed me a just-picked bouquet of daffodils,
said she got them in the neighbor's yard.

Lollapaloser

So your second marriage
is not sad.
You are not drunk
on half a bottle of warm Zima
and your children
are at home cleaning their rooms.
You are not parked in a mud hole
twenty miles up Coos River
listening to Dwight Yoakam's
A Thousand Miles From Nowhere.
You are not in any pain
and no one has ever done you wrong.
You have never suffered
from carpal tunnel syndrome,
bled irregularly,
or survived a butt-first breech delivery
when your first child was born
just prior to
C-sections becoming commonplace.
You refuse to feel sorry
for thirty-eight-year-old
mid-life crisis participants
who find themselves temporarily
in love with any child who looks lost
or any man who looks lonely.
You have never had a cold heart
or a weak faith.

You are not drunk.
No one has ever done you wrong
and oh sure
you knew
that your father was only teasing
about your being the milkman's daughter.

Warning

My sister tells me that people see it.
Men, especially.
It's that little lost look of yours,
saying you're not quite happy. In fact,
she says, I'd go so far as to say you project it.
I know it's unintentional.
You're a dedicated wife.
And when people see
your commitment to God
they're in awe of you. But
I'm telling you, she says, you've always had
that look, and, that figure —
the best figure of all us girls —
that waist, that butt,
and those eyes.

Almost

I forget
that I'm a stepmother,
that my stepdaughter's not
quite mine,
that I have an ex
who married my ex-best friend,
that they have a baby daughter now.
I forget
that I'm living in a half-world.
My son,
when he laughs out loud
or tips his head to one side, almost profile,
looks exactly like his father.

Sister Ritual

Every morning I
call Mary Beth, Bob Etta, and Donna June. Usually I
call Mary Beth first. When her phone's busy I
call Bob Etta. If she's busy I
know she's probably talking to Mary Beth, so I
call Donna June. If her phone's busy I
figure she's trying to call me, so I
hang up. Wait a second. Push redial. If I
get a second busy signal I
try Mary Beth / Bob Etta again. If they're still busy I
call Tana Rae long distance. If she's busy I
eat breakfast.

This Poem

Some minor family crisis last night
that I've already put walls up around.
Some little denial game probably,
the way my legs are crossed at the knees
with my right foot wrapped tight
around my left ankle, pretzel-like,
to where it would be too much trouble
to untwist and reach across the stack of self-help books
in order to change my radio's station
which apparently has been switched from blues to gospel
by some family member who knows
I'd rather not have them messing around my writing desk.
The wrong music can throw you off track. Or maybe
it's my unmade bed, the dust on my banker's lamp,
or this foggy August morning. Maybe
it's trying to write serious poetry
when you're out of Kotex and your coffee's cold. Maybe
it's trying to convince yourself that you are not this poem,
that there will be a surprise line that you didn't know
you had in you. Maybe it's my sister
who's been diagnosed with inoperable cancer. Maybe
it's having solid white hair years before turning forty,
Nice 'n Easy's copper auburn stains
under your fingernails every month.
Or the way my legs are crossed, my toes turning blue.

Carrots In The Rain

I'm in the driver's seat
of my sister's '78 Ford
because she can't see to drive
after dark. A whole carload of us
has just come from visiting our dad
who's dying with liver cirrhosis
and terminal stubbornness.
I'm waiting with four sisters and one aunt
in an almost empty restaurant parking lot
for another sister to get off work,
the sister who's recovering from cancer
while washing dishes at the local greasy spoon.
We see her coming from around back and holler,
Hey, Tana Rae!
She has this little square styrofoam container,
she opens it up and asks if we want a carrot.
She gives us each one. We crunch and talk,
decide to go somewhere for coffee.
Leaning against the car's passenger door,
Tana Rae digs in her purse for her keys
because she can't fit in our car with us. We laugh.
Sitting scrunched in the old Ford crunching
our leftover crinkle cut carrots, we laugh.
It starts to rain. Waving her carrot stub wildly,
one back seat sister leans forward
and asks if I'm gonna write a poem about this.

Good News

I've got to write a letter, card or something, anything,
to the cutest, sweetest married couple I've ever known
who took me and my boys in when I divorced and had my
    hell year.
I read in the paper today that they've filed for divorce.

Oh the beautiful car
that I practically gave away to my youngest son
that got its whole front end smashed when he hit that deer
on Highway 38, cruising at about 75 mph.

I get away to drink a triple shot mocha
with two writer friends, one of whom has a brain tumor.

Then there's my dad, desperate with no pain medication,
dying at home. He broke his ankle last week. He offered
me six hundred dollars to stay with him till he dies.

I've got a pap test scheduled for next Tuesday,
sure enough, the same day my sister starts her chemotherapy.
Good news: my oldest sister checked,
found out that the local American Cancer Society
will fit her with a wig, one that matches her hair color,
and give her a couple of turbans for free.

Growing Old Near Charleston

I'm still a Fossil Point kid,
poking stiff seaweed
into pale green anemone,
prying starfish over onto their backs.
I'm still afraid of half-dead crabs.

I remember crashing into cold waves
at Sunset Beach, in fog, barefoot —
because my sister did —
and spitting salt water.
We bought taffy at the Shell Shop,
Charleston Chews at Davey Jones Locker,
and candy cigarettes at Barview Store.

Wearing warmer clothes these days,
I watch waves break from my car window,
eat clam chowder and drink coffee.
Sunny days I search for whole sand dollars
and blue beach glass,
finding only broken pieces.

Bunny Arkansas Days

I want to write about Bob Etta,
Donna June, Gary Lee, Tana Rae, Mary Beth and me.
I want to write about Bunny Arkansas days,
Gideon Missouri, Flint Michigan, and Tenmile Oregon.
I want the cat off my lap, my dishes done, my headache gone.
I want my husband's fishing pole off the dining table,
his sandshrimp back in the sand.
I want my oven cleaned,
my kitchen floor mopped.
I want somebody else
to pick up every single pile of dog crap in the back yard.

I want to write about Olalla Road, Pierce Point,
blackberries and possums.
I want to know why
I let my sisters talk me into helping them move my
        antique dresser
out of one sister's house —
I can't believe I let her have it in the first place —
and up into the back of my husband's very high
        four-wheel-drive truck,
then across town to another sister's house, all the way up
her stairs, then sideways into her tiny bathroom,
only to have her decide that it doesn't look quite right,
        then back
down the stairs, back up into the truck

to finally wind up back where it started — my house,
where it no longer fits because I of course replaced its
    empty space
with another dresser.

I want both dressers.
I want a bigger house.
I want to trade my '84 Ford
straight across for Bob Etta's '91 Prelude.
My husband wants some other family member to own
    a pickup truck.

PART THREE:
WHAT THE CLEANING LADY KNOWS

What The Cleaning Lady Knows

Cleanliness is not and never has been next to godliness.

White carpets are hell.

You can get by without Comet, Spic and Span or lemon oil,
but Windex is mandatory.

Ammonia can cause pneumonia.

People who pay to have clean houses cleaned are lonely.

Children whose parents work full-time will fall in love with you.

Rich people splatter diarrhea
on the inside rim of their toilet seats, just like the rest of us.

Cleaning rags should always be washed separately with
    bleach.

Cash is better than checks.

Down On My Knees

cleaning out my refrigerator
and thinking about writing a religious poem
that somehow combines feeling sorry for myself
with ordinary praise, when my nephew stumbles in for coffee
to wash down what looks like a hangover
and get rid of what he calls hot dog water breath.
I wasn't going to bake the cake

now cooling on the counter, but I found a dozen eggs tipped
sideways in their carton behind a leftover Thanksgiving
    Jell-O dish.
There's something therapeutic about baking a devil's
    food cake,
whipping up that buttercream frosting,
knowing your sisters will drop by and say Lord yes
they'd love just a little piece.

Everybody suffers, wants to run away,
is broke after Christmas, stayed up too late
to make it to church Sunday morning. Everybody should

drink coffee with their nephews,
eat chocolate cake with their sisters, be thankful
and happy enough under a warm and unexpected January sun.

Dear Dad

I wish I was there with you
drinking weak coffee, eating cheese,
crackers, canned tuna, pork rinds,
and pickled pig's feet.

I want to sit with you
on the old back porch, chain-smoke
generic cigarettes till we fill
every tuna fish can ashtray you own.

We could talk about Momma,
all the women you've known since
she's been gone, argue a bit
about religion, sex, drugs, and diabetes.

I wouldn't mention your desperate need
to see a doctor, because I know
how much you hate the sonofabitches.

Instead I'd say you look good
for a lonely, dried-up, 73-year-old man
who admits he would have taken
far better care of himself if he'd known
he was gonna live this long.

I miss Dillard, Dad. I miss Roseburg, Winston,
the swimmin' hole at Coon Hollow,

the South Umpqua River, stealing watermelons
from Burk's Blue Fruit Stand on hot summer nights,
and picking beans to help pay for school clothes.

All your North Bend/Coos Bay kids
are fine, and keeping plenty busy.
Monday I cleaned the church building,
Tuesday I cleaned at home. Wednesday
I taught a children's Bible class,
tonight I have a class. But come Friday

I'll be happy on Highway 42,
passing chip trucks in the rain, swerving
to miss mud slides, stopping in Remote
to get rid of coffee so I can buy more, and singing
with the radio, cruising through Camas Valley,
hanging a right at Brockway Store...

Home Alone

Cigarette smokers,
sweet tooths,
alcoholics, teetotalers,
bad cooks, good cooks,
food stamp recipients,
low blood sugar and type 2 diabetes,
depression, codependency, cancer,
high energy, low self-esteem,
nap takers, neat freaks, control freaks,
carpal tunnel syndrome,
strong arms, skinny ankles, pot bellies,
public speakers, introverts, braggers,
blue eyes, long legs, red necks,
enablers, naggers, whiners,
pride, guilt and honesty all run in my family.
We have an out of work long haul truck driver,
a race car driver, a certified pesticide applicator,
an Olympic decathlon pole vault record breaker,
Sunday School teachers, a politician, a poet,
professional house cleaners, a dishwasher who
works in a dive for dimes, and an Environmental
Services worker who mops floors at the local hospital
and recently moved in with me because
paying off her ex's bills put her in a real bind and
even though she comes in from work exhausted
she manages to vacuum my carpets and Comet my toilets.
There's never a dull moment, though I'm praying for one,

that my sister will get her own place soon,
that my brilliant, eighteen-year-old needs-to-get-a-job son
will snap out of it, that my in-laws place will hurry up
    and sell,
that they'll pack up and move to Arkansas already....
    I see myself
home alone writing a poem in a quiet house, smoking one
    cigarette
after another, eating candy, flicking
my ashes on the floor.

Mikey Likes It

the way I wait on him
hand and foot, wash his hair
most mornings, fry up hashbrowns,
mend his work jeans and in general
act interested even when I'm not.
Mikey likes back rubs, "Renegade" reruns,
race cars, fishing poles, guns,
beef jerky and a beefed-up truck.
He doesn't do dishes or yard work. He forgets
my birthday and doesn't bring me flowers.
No candy. No sweet talk. But I know
he loves me. He pays the bills,
gives my grown boys bear hugs
and money when he sees a need.
Once he charged a new set of tires
for my sister's old car
because she's alone and poor.
If you need a place to stay,
Mikey will give you our key.

If He's Lucky

When his lower back goes out
Dad will lie down flat
on his living room floor,
raise his legs up
as high as he can
     (his hernia tucks back
into his groin),
and kind of swivel his feet
first one way, then the other, slowly.
If he's lucky
his pain goes away.

Frail, beanpole thin,
Dad thinks about dying.
He calls up the mental list of his life,
good things to one side,
bad things to the other, believing
the good outweighs the bad.
For just a moment
he thinks he'll make it
into heaven
as he lies there
feeling no pain,
his cold hands folded
across his heart,
his feet up,
his eyes closed.

Old Bawling Hags

Lonely, horny, divorced,
a struggling, gross Christian
recently prescribed antibiotics
and nerve pills, hooked on nicotine,
caffeine and non-dairy creamer,
my sister says she's willing
to lower her standards, date a man
ugly as a mud fence
or stupid as a box of rocks,
so long as he has a kind heart.

Parked at a downtown 7-Eleven,
we share chili cheese nachos,
a Big Gulp, and a buy-two-
get-one-free pack of Sno Balls.
Counting each other's gray hair and wrinkles,
we split a Moon Pie and cry.

Pre-Holiday PMS

I don't want to be thankful this year.
I don't want to eat turkey and I could care
if I never again tasted
your mother's cornbread stuffing.
I hate sweet potato pie. I hate mini marshmallows.
I hate doing dishes while you watch football.

I hate Christmas. I hate name-drawing.
I hate tree-trimming, gift-wrapping,
and Rudolph the zipper-necked red-nosed reindeer.
I just want to skip the whole merry mess—
unless, of course, you'd like to try
to change my mind. You could start
by telling me I'm pretty and leaving me
your charge cards
and all your cash.

Sleeping With Dad

I was in the seventh grade.
That dark-haired woman from Coos Bay
and her two pretty but wicked teenage daughters
had finally moved out. I have no idea
where my sister Mary Beth had gone off to.
This was the year she started drinking.
I hated our tiny dark back bedroom, was afraid
to sleep alone in it.
Early evening, Dad slid the couch
out from the wall, let the back down, click.
The nerve
in Dad's lower back was pinched, and he said
he'd have to sleep on the couch for a few nights
because his bed springs were shot.
If you want, he said, unfolding the brown wool blanket,
you can sleep with me.

In the cold dark,
with all my clothes on, I slipped under
the scratchy wool, slowly inched toward him until
my toes were against the backs of his calves, my nose,
somewhere between his shoulder blades
smelling his musty stinky T-shirt smell.
For one long, wonderful week —
that smell I'd never before liked, that touch
I'd always wanted.

Menopause

I dreamed I had an alligator belly,
washboard hard. We're talking Schwarzenegger.
Now I've had my share of odd dreams,
gross dreams I've never told anyone about.
I've had nightmares that sat me straight up
and left every light in the house on.
I've had trapped in hell dreams,
a shopping downtown naked dream.
Never had a flying dream though,
and I think I'd like that.
Anyhow, I called my sister
and told her about my buffed belly dream,
how my fingers still felt numb from rubbing it over and
        over again,
how I felt scared and wondered what my friends would think.
My sister, who's in her second year of major menopause, said,
Oh Ginger Gay, that's nothing! I could fill buckets
with the sweat from all my horror dreams —
and you're calling *me* with a silly little hard belly dream?
It's nothing, trust me! Just put a shirt over it and get here
        quick
to help me cut off this huge, bloody growth
hanging out of my crotch.

Sadder Than A Beautiful
Young Woman

with money,
a good man,
and cancer,
is my not so young,
not so beautiful sister
who's flat broke,
divorced
and has cancer.

Saddest of all is the fact
that I pussyfoot around
telling her that it's never too late
to let go and let God.
Wouldn't want to preach
her a sermon or anything.

I Punch Out Jesus,

Peter, Andrew, James, John,
the empty net, and the net full of fish
from the visual aids packet
for my pre-schoolers' next Sunday School lesson.

> *Questions:*
> *What were the fishermen doing when Jesus first*
> *saw them?*
> *How many fish had they caught?*
> *What happened when Jesus told Peter to throw his*
> *net into the water?*
> The kids will know the answers.

Tell me again about forever,
about that land of endless day,
that part about no pain,
no tears.

My Sister Believes In Miracles

The latest of which
is a short, bald, fifty-year-old Italian
with sciatic nerve damage in his left leg
resulting from his second or is it his third back surgery.
He's wonderful. They're a perfect match she tells me,
what with both of them being recovered
alcoholic / drug addicts, both
on the wagon for years now, both
having named their Higher Power. God, of course,
who first had to teach her once and for all
the heartbreak of lust combined with low self-esteem,
followed by the proverbial codependent marriage
and the subsequent births of children
she has no control over, whose fathers
are worthless, nowhere to be found
when their little girls cry in the middle of the night.
She's met his family, all responsible
come-from-old-money Italians.
One younger brother she says is drop-dead gorgeous.
It's crazy. It's amazing, she says,
a German marrying an Italian.
A neat freak versus a slob.
He makes his children mind.
He owns three cars, she says. Three!
He wants to pay my phone bill for God's sake.
Neither of us can cook.
He doesn't drink any more.
He believes in Jesus.

Backflip

There are the beautifully wind-deformed pine trees
just at the edge of the cliffs here. And, the ocean —
its secret beaches I've been going to tell about
for the longest time now. Sand dollars, fat jellyfish,
anemone, yellow scotch broom in bloom, beach grass, stinky
seaweed, snails on salal leaves, hundreds of tiny sand fleas
    doing backflips.
There are so many wind, sand, and ocean-swept clean
    things. There is

my ex brother-in-law sitting cross-legged on my living
    room floor
watching the local morning news, killing time before walking
in the rain to my oldest sister's house. He's going to build a
    deck for her.
We all still love him, find odd jobs for him when he's in town.
He's still almost good-looking, but way too thin. He's lost
all his front teeth. He's finally off drugs, a beer drinker now.
Some days, he says, he'll go through half a case by noon.

Going Down

I'm scrubbing my back bathroom toilet
Because you never know when
Someone might stop by
And need to use it just when
Someone else has the main bath occupied.
It could happen.
I can't believe that my sister,
My best friend,
Married that old tightwad Italian
And moved away. I might as well
Scrub the tub while I'm on my knees.
My sister did call last week. She'd
Just come from visiting our dad
Who's still refusing medication
But wishes he had some more of those percodans
Like they gave him before
They amputated his leg. She said
Dad checked his blood sugar level
And it was up again, sky high.
He just wants to be left alone.
I can't believe the mold
That's grown on the tile grout back here.
God. What a mess. That's me,
Straightening deck chairs on the Titanic,
Lining those loungers up perfect,
When there's souls to be saved,
And the ship is going down.

With A Wicked Little Jab

I stop / eject the Golden Oldies cassette
of Jerry Lee Lewis singing *"goodness gracious,
great balls of fire."* I'm not in the mood
for a blast from the past or even the two bites of
    old-fashioned
microwaved oatmeal that I knew I couldn't eat
before I cooked it. I just wanted to act routine,
take a shower, get dressed, eat something, dust a
    bookcase, burn
some paper trash, thank God for my day off.
Thought I'd clean out a closet, or maybe bake cookies.
But I can still feel yesterday's sun, yesterday's headache,
the way I had the nerve to whine about it
to whatever sister stood by me in our dad's yard as we
    watched
our brother mow the wet grass,
a cigarette hanging out of the corner of his mouth,
the way the mower kept dying, the way he patiently
bent down with a stick, tipped the mower
to knock clumped grass off the dull blades,
while, white-faced, our dad was throwing up
off the corner of the front porch, sitting bent over
in his wheel chair, trying not to get any on his one foot.
He wants us to believe that his surgeon saws off legs for
    money.
He's fired his diabetes doctor, hasn't had insulin for days,
thinks Home Health care is a joke,

and told the Meals on Wheels folks to hit the road.
He says he wants to be alone. But
he gets scared, calls us up. So we come to mow his yard
and cook him meals that he can't keep down.
He wants to die at home.
And he wants us there when it happens.

Habitual Offender

My oldest sister sits
eating a cracker at our dad's kitchen table.
Dad's false leg with its worn, black shoe,
lace undone, stands beside her next to the wall
by the window where gray light manages
to filter through the three-quarters shut miniblinds
stained yellow with cigarette smoke and gas fumes
from his stove's burners
which keep his little shack house way too hot. But Dad
says he'll never be warm again.
Our eyes burn and water every time we visit. Every weekend.
But, after twenty minutes or so, our eyes adjust,
and it's not so bad.
His drinking water smells.
We bring in bottled water for coffee, hide it under his sink
so we won't have to listen to him gripe
about how he's been drinking his water for going on
        twenty-six years now.
Diabetic ulcers have formed on the bottom and side
of his one foot. His toes are purple.
He suffered too much with his first amputation, he says,
to live through another one.
He's sleeping now. So we sit. My sister hands out
crackers, puts on some coffee. I'm wondering
if our brother will show up, but I'm thinking
he's holed up somewhere half-drunk, crying
in his beer, forty-five years old, waiting
for his old man to just once tell him that he loves him.

PART FOUR:
NOT SLEEPING TOO GOOD MYSELF

Thanksgiving

"Do not forget to entertain strangers, for by so doing some people have entertained angels without knowing it."
—Hebrews 13:2

If the almost perfectly fluted edge
of your homemade pumpkin pie's crust burns
even though you carefully crinkled aluminum foil
    around it
as soon as you noticed it was browning way too fast,
for goodness sake don't cry. Just cut it off.
Swirl Cool Whip around where the crust was.
Nobody really cares. They will eat it.
Life will go on, trust me. The truth is
There's always someone with a sadder story.

If your father hasn't had both of his legs amputated,
if he isn't lying on a pee-stained mattress;
doesn't have bed sores, a diaper rash, a shriveling liver,
a bad heart and cataracts; if your sister
isn't burnt black from neck to groin
from radiation, if chemo
doesn't have her full of phlegm and bile, trust me,
these are your good times.

The trick is keeping busy, cleaning house, cooking, opening
your door to strangers, entertaining all possible angels.

No Code*

I'm thankful that my brother wasn't drunk
when he found our dad dead in his own smelly bed.
My sister, coming in through the back door,
saw Dad dead first, but just kept walking
straight through to the kitchen to put on coffee, open
    curtains.
I'm thankful that my sister wasn't drunk,
that she's been sober for ten years now. Thank God.
Thank God it was my brother who closed Dad's eyes,
who called the appropriate authorities, chatting calmly
with my sister over coffee while they waited.

*A prearranged agreement for no life support

Not Sleeping Too Good Myself

My sister slips up and lets out
That she's on sleeping pills.
Her welfare caseworker referred her to Mental Health.
They set her up with this counselor who
Prescribed 15mg. of flurazepam. Not sleeping
Too good myself, I'm thrilled for her.
The State seems plenty worried
About her getting a job — she looks like death,
Both her father and a sister have recently died,
She's married to, but not living with,
Some Catholic-Italian-Mafia-type.
They've convinced her that she's abusing her body,
Told her to try cutting down on caffeine,
And to eat a regular meal at least once a day.

She tells me that she's told them about God.
I'm not surprised. My sister, the caretaker:
Finally taking better care of herself, eating
Some hot meals, drinking way less coffee, sleeping
Half the night, putting in job applications, inviting
Her caseworker to come to church some Sunday.

I Try Not To Write Poems

about my dead sister's daughter's blocked fallopian tubes,
About how badly she wants to have a baby
But can't afford the corrective surgery right now.
Funerals are expensive.

I try not to write
About family, death,
Cancer, divorce, my nephew's autistic son, alcoholism,
Hepatitis C, insomnia, root canals — my dentist says I
　　need two, or
I could have both teeth pulled and see an orthodontist, maybe
Get a partial.

I try not to think
About money, how I don't have enough
To pay for my son's careless driving ticket.
From a thousand miles away he tells me not to worry,
That he's too busy with Technical Writing to be driving
　　anyway.
He's going to a Christian college to become an engineer
So that he can make lots of money and some day
Buy his momma a summer home by a lake somewhere
　　beautiful and peaceful

Where I could write poetry all day long.

After My Tenth Death Poem In A Row

I tell myself that I've got to stop this, get out
In a green meadow somewhere and talk to some dandelions,
Roll around in the grass, careful
Not to squish any little living thing.
Here's a long title for poem number eleven:
    "Accidentally Killing Some Little Bugs
    When I Was Just Trying To Get Away
    From It All And Lie Down In A Quiet Meadow..."
Well, it isn't going to happen. I don't have time to get away
Because I've taken on extra work so I won't have time
    to think
About my dead sister and father and everybody
Knows there is no clear escape from death — unless
God's got your name in the Book of Life. But I am not dead,
And after so many days I am no longer bawling
In grocery store aisles, and have actually begun to laugh
At stupid jokes on TV sitcoms.
Oh, I can keep writing death if I want to. I can feel sorry
For the little bugs, the ten or twelve out of however many
    zillions
That I might kill in some green place sometime if I want to.

Smoking and Drinking

Dad warns me
That there are approximately fourteen farts per cup of coffee.
But it's very important, he says, to get any and all poison
Build up out of a body. It's nothing to be ashamed of.
Your straight shot of whiskey'll kill germs. Cigarette smoke
Is good too. It keeps bugs and general impurities out of
     the air.
And if it weren't for his baseball-sized hernia popping out
Every time he lights up, he'd still be rolling his own.

Dad says he doesn't worry about anything.
When he goes to bed at night, he sleeps.
He tells me to get a second opinion
Before I go getting cut on for any female problems.
All doctors are quacks, he says. Look at how many times
They've tried to kill me. Look how they killed your mother.

Time and Money

Monday. March 10th. Exactly
Two months since my sister died
And I'm depressed over how depressed I still am.
My husband asks what's the matter and I tell him
For God's sake it's only been two months.
He doesn't know what he can do for me,
So he chops kindling.
He's chopped enough to last well into winter.
I tell him it's not just death, it's everything —
My crappy cleaning jobs, my arthritis, my fuzzy perm.
Don't you ever feel old, I ask, don't you ever feel
Bad about your thinning hair? Nope, he says.
Doesn't bother me at all.
The sooner it all falls out the better.
Same with my teeth.

Corns And Bunions

Certainly, bunions are painful, hard
To live with, the reality of never again
Wearing your favorite high heels
Or any pretty shoes for that matter.
Oh my beautiful dresses,
My silky, slinky things that
Will now look as stupid as goose manure,
Worn with ugly, flat, wide shoes.
There is a surgical procedure for bunions, but I'm chicken.
I'll just go orthopedic. Well, I shouldn't say just—
For Pete's sake, I'm only 40. Well, maybe I shouldn't say
Only. My mother died at 42. She didn't have bunions,
but she did have corns.

O Momma

I come from a real life
soap opera family
complete with death,
replacements, affairs, adoptions, abortions,
addicts, prison terms, love, etcetera.

They say we're a kind bunch
helping each other, and anyone hurting.
I think it's death
that's brought us so close.
Especially Momma's.

I remember Dad raising
the bushy eyebrow over his one good eye,
and telling us to be careful
of seeing only the good side of people.

But we're perceptive that way.
We know hurt.

Stuff

I was thinking it was just me with my
little ongoing sadnesses, regrets and poor life choices
combined with a sinus infection and PMS,
but it's looking like everybody is on the verge
of tears. Here I am, bloated, just waiting to start
bleeding like a stuck pig, with swollen eyelids
and nasal passages, praying for a post nasal drip,
with a huge pimple right in the middle of my forehead —
the kind you know better than to squeeze, smiling
anyway, when people around me are crying.
Well, some with just their eyes full, blinking rapidly.
Men, women, children, family, friends, fellow Christians —
the normally on-top-of-things people are falling apart,
        breaking
down in front of me. Folks who've made good choices,
have good jobs, money to send their kids to private schools,
the best colleges. Women I know who are as pretty
on the inside as the outside, are crying to *me* for God's sake.
Do they think I have it together or something?
Is it my kind heart? Is that my problem? Don't they know
I'm a poet, that I'll write this stuff down?

The Gift

The preacher's sermon is on the parable of the talents.
His point is that God has given each of us at least one gift.
The challenge is to know what our gifts are.

Recovering from her third divorce,
a former bartender, a heavy smoker,
eater of half a dozen donuts at a time,
loudmouthed, interruptive,
big-hearted and God-fearing,
my sister says she knows what her one talent is:
Encouraging others.

God Comes in Handy

when you're recently divorced,
Oh so vulnerable, yet thankful
That you're nowhere near as lost as you once were,
Licking the couple of dandruff-like flakes of crank
Off your tongue-dampened finger
Because your nose is too raw to snort up
That last little bit.
When you're walking with your head down
Years later, clean and brutally sober,
When out of the clear blue
You practically step on this little square
Half gram of the stuff, chopped and ready,
Right there in your own front yard,
At the tip of your worn-out Reebok,
Glowing up out of the green grass.
Of course nobody is around,
So you pocket it. Stunned.
Down on your luck and money,
You know you could sell it,
Buy your mixed-up child new school clothes,
Pay your phone bill, or just portion it out
And mix it with your coffee
For who knows how many mornings.
Energy. Power! Yeah, right.
                              Shaky,
Your face pale in the mirror above the toilet,
You drop the shit and flush.

Crazy 'Bout a Mercury

As you know, my sister says, I talk to God
about everything. Lately I've talked a lot
about being poor, how I don't like it. Sure,
I know I'm not *really* poor, but, the thing is —
I know you already know this —
if you're with Him, He overlooks
your weaknesses whatever they may be,
mine being greed and sex, as in, I want some
but can't have it right now. Sure, it's my own fault
for picking drunks and druggies for husbands, anyway
I got to thinking about that Mustard Seed Faith,
how Jesus says, I tell you the truth,
if you have faith the size of a mustard seed
you can move mountains. Well,
you know how I've had nothing
but a string of junker cars that break down, blow up,
    catch on fire,
and it struck me that all I gotta do is ask for a decent car.
If I asked for a brand spanking new Mercury,
I know God would give me one. Now
I'm not saying I'm gonna ask Him,
I figure I got a couple hundred miles left in my old
    Plymouth,
and, I'm learning to pray for what I really need,
not just for what I think I want, like sex.

A Man For Mary

One who wouldn't dream of insisting
that she pay her own car insurance,
buy her own food, and have sex every night
whether she's bathed or not.

A divorced man is OK —
she's divorced herself, three times.
She used to drink, do drugs.
She was beaten once, locked up
for three nights.

Mary wants a Stable Sam kind of guy, a God-fearing
responsible man who's got a house
she could help make a home. Maybe
one of those newer manufactured homes, but
she's had it with eighteen-foot tin cans that leak.

Mary loves house plants, lots of windows, lots of light.

December Sunday

Two of my sisters and I decide to skip Bible study
And drive to Roseburg in time to catch the worship
Services there, then go visit our unstable, still recovering
From Dad's death, still alcoholic brother, whom we love.
We stop for coffee, stop for gas, stop to use the sani-cans
At the covered bridge in Remote. We don't make it
In time for church. When we get to our brother's,
I fall asleep in his recliner.
He's hoping to come see us next weekend. He gives us
     the key
To our dad's place, a rundown shack we've put up for sale.
We go home the long way to stop there
To get Dad's old orange hanging lamps for our niece.
She says they'll look perfect in her condominium.
We pick up cheeseburger baskets, decide to eat them at
     Dad's,
Like we used to, sitting around the dark brown Formica-
Chipped kitchen table with the green chairs.

The back door still sticks.
The kitchen faucet still drips.
We can still smell mold and urine.
It's so cold we see our breath.
Steam rises from our French-fries.
I mention that I'm just not feeling too well, probably
Getting that flu. My sisters can't get the hanging lamps
To come loose from the living room ceiling. It looks like

Dad screwed the stupid things up too tight. Maybe,
If the place doesn't sell, come spring
We'll come back and figure out how
To unscrew the ugly things, get them down
Without tearing them up.

Sometimes a Cleaning Lady

gets to feeling sorry for herself, her reflection these days
in somebody else's floor-to-ceiling,
beveled, cherrywood framed to-die-for mirror,
her forty-something year-old not-so-blue anymore eyes,
the tiny purple broken veins on either side of her nose
that her pan stick makeup conceals only until
she begins perspiring in the indoor August heat;
her head in somebody else's oven, her toilet brush
scouring some rich retired doctor's mauve toilet
whose pale color exactly matches the tile
surrounding the large oval shaped Jacuzzi
with its gold faucets, spigot, and drain;
as she wipes the tiny blonde shaved hairs
stuck three quarters up the side of the tub, gently,
with Soft Scrub, so as not to scratch the surface.

She knows that she is trusted.
She knows that money and things
don't necessarily make you happy or prettier,
that she could turn
on the air conditioning, make herself
a sandwich if she wanted to. You wouldn't
believe what all she knows. Today she found a note
left on top of her check: Help yourself to a cold drink,
      Sweetheart,
make yourself at home.

For everyone who exalts himself will be humbled, and he who humbles himself will be exalted. —Luke 14:11